"Are you all right?" he asked in concern. "Are you sick?"

"I. . .I. . ." She began to back away. "I. . .you look so familiar."

He laughed. "Wish I could say you did, too, but I'd be telling a tall tale." He chuckled again.

Oh, dear God, have You brought Eric back to life? Is this real? Did something strange happen? A miracle maybe? Or had he come back, and now he had amnesia or something? "Is your name Eric?" she suddenly blurted out.

"What? No. I'm Anson." He held out his hand. She made a feeble attempt to grasp it before her hand fell away. "Have we met?"

"I–I'm sorry." She spun about and hurried away. When she turned back to look, the man was walking in the opposite direction. He then turned, too. Their gazes met. *Dear God, what am I going to do? It's like he's come back. Eric's alive! But. . . he's dead. We buried him.*

Didn't we?

LAURALEE BLISS, a former nurse, is a prolific writer of inspirational fiction as well as a home educator. She resides with her family near Charlottesville, Virginia, in the foothills of the Blue Ridge Mountains—a place of inspiration for many of her contemporary and historical novels. Lauralee Bliss writes inspirational fiction to provide readers with entertaining stories intertwined with Christian principles to assist them in their day-to-day walk with the Lord. Aside from writing, she enjoys gardening, cross-stitching, reading, roaming yard sales, and traveling. Lauralee invites you to visit her Web site at http://www.lauraleebliss.com.

Books by Lauralee Bliss

HEARTSONG PRESENTS

Don't miss out on any of our super romances. Write to us at the following address for information on our newest releases and club information.

Heartsong Presents Readers' Service
PO Box 721
Uhrichsville, OH 44683

Or visit www.heartsongpresents.com

Heart of Mine

Lauralee Bliss

Heartsong Presents

To JoAnne, Margie, and Rachel for making my very rough draft of an idea a real book. Thanks so much for all you do.

A note from the Author:
I love to hear from my readers! You may correspond with me by writing:

Lauralee Bliss
Author Relations
PO Box 721
Uhrichsville, OH 44683

ISBN 978-1-60260-913-6

HEART OF MINE

All scripture quotations are taken from the HOLY BIBLE, NEW INTERNATIONAL VERSION ® . NIV ®. Copyright © 1973, 1978, 1984 by International Bible Society. Used by permission of Zondervan. All rights reserved.

All of the characters and events in this book are fictitious. Any resemblance to actual persons, living or dead, or to actual events is purely coincidental.

Our mission is to publish and distribute inspirational products offering exceptional value and biblical encouragement to the masses.

PRINTED IN THE U.S.A.

one

So many questions and so little in the way of answers. Marissa Jones tried not to let it grate on her, but the constant day in, day out pondering was wearing her down. She shifted her cell phone to the other ear while throwing more books into a box. "Mom, remember, the caterer told me the deposit was forfeited. Don't worry, I handled it months ago." Pause. "Yes, I did read the fine print when I signed the contract." She wanted to add, *And how was I to know that Eric would die? Why are we talking about this? There are so many other things that we need to discuss. Like my move back home.* She bit her lip, refusing to say what she thought—Mom was being difficult once again.

"Why are you so short with me?" Mom went on. "I know it's been hard, but we need to make sure everything is set."

Marissa believed she had good reason to be on the sour side of things. After all, she'd lost her fiancé several months ago. Life had been turned on its head. Now she was about to move back to her hometown of Cedar City, Utah. Leave Nebraska and its memories. "I'm sorry. Look, I know you're only trying to help me tie up loose ends."

"Well, it's good you're coming back here. You were never the same when you left. Really, ever since you left for college and then moved so far away. You changed so much."

Yes, I've changed. In ways I never thought I would. Who wouldn't, when your fiancé dies unexpectedly a month before the wedding?

But she had to wonder, too, if Mom held some hidden

5

thankfulness that things turned out the way they did. After all, Mom had been lonely since she and Dad divorced. She never wanted her and her sister Phyllis to move away. "Who will I go shopping with?" she'd mourned. "Who will I eat with?" But in time, it seemed Mom had overcome much in her life. And maybe they could do a little reconnecting now that it was just the two of them, without a husband or fiancé.

"Marissa, are you still there? Oh, how I hate these cell phones. I never know if someone has a decent connection or not. Betty uses one all the time, and then suddenly she's gone. I'll be talking away and find out she hadn't heard a thing I'd said."

"Yes, Mom, I'm still here. Hey, I'm sorry, but I have some more packing to do before the movers get here. I'll give you a call before I leave."

"Well, all right. You sure you're still coming? You won't change your mind or anything?"

Marissa thought she detected worry in her mom's voice. "Yes, I'll be there. Trust me. I've packed up everything."

When the call ended, she thought to herself, *I'll never be more thankful to leave here. I see Eric everywhere.* She forced away the tears that tried to well up. *Sometimes I think I hear his voice. Smell his cologne. I hear the cell phone ring and think it's him. And of course, all his friends and family are here. It's time to move on. And Cedar City is the place I believe God wants me to be.*

Marissa consoled herself these last few weeks by preparing for the move. Six months had passed since Eric's death, yet the memories were too raw. It was difficult enough having to drive by the church where she was supposed to get married or the fancy hotel they had booked for the reception. She'd sold her wedding gown on craigslist. She had yet to take off her engagement ring. She stared at it even now—an exquisite one-carat diamond set in solid gold. Eric never went cheap when it came to what she wanted. From jewelry to bouquets of flowers on their engagement anniversaries to an iPod one day as a surprise gift. At least she could look at the engagement ring without tears welling up in her eyes. Maybe it was a sign her heart was on the mend; that she was ready for this move. No longer did she feel paralyzed by her circumstances. The door was open, and she intended to walk through with her head held high and her emotions held in check.

Marissa continued to load up a box. Many things had already been packed into boxes, ready for her and Eric to begin their life together, when the terrible news came. He'd been in a car wreck out on the interstate and was killed instantly at the scene. She recalled how everything went into slow motion in those terrible days that followed. The parade of sympathy in the form of calls, casseroles, and cards. The funeral where Marissa sat without family, while all of Eric's family and friends were there, consoling each other. The lonely times that followed. It was then she realized how important family was in tough times. And friends, too. Like the friends she'd left behind from the church youth group in Cedar City. Denise and Joy. Last she'd heard they were still around, though Joy had recently gotten married. And of course, Mom had all her friends.

Cedar City was a good place to be, as it was nothing like Omaha. The town was small, filled with touristy-type places like the historic downtown and array of shops. Unlike Omaha's river bluffs, Cedar City was surrounded by the natural beauty of red rock canyons, hoodoos, rivers, and even a mountain that provided skiing in the winter. But she wasn't returning for all that. She was going back to discover new things. A new purpose. Perhaps new love. And Utah held plenty of interesting memories. High school, prom, an old boyfriend, ski trips, even college where she met Eric for the first time. Utah had memories but not the painful feelings like here in Omaha. It was a place to start fresh.

The cell phone played a tune once more. Mom again. Marissa groaned. "I'm never going to get this packing done...."

"Oh Marissa, I have the most wonderful news! I just got off the phone with Betty Newberry. You must remember her, I'm sure. Well, she and I are in the craft club together. And guess who's also moving back to Cedar City? Just in time for your arrival!"

"Who's that, Mom?" She tried positioning the phone on her shoulder so she could wrap glasses in tufts of newspaper.

"Wayne. Betty's son. Remember him from high school?"

Wayne Newberry. She hadn't heard that name in a long time. Memories rose to the surface, of a tall guy with thick, wavy hair who was voted most successful in the high school yearbook. They'd dated a few times. And he was her prom date. "What about Wayne?"

"He's coming back to Cedar City to set up his practice. He's a successful psychologist according to Betty. He helps people with their problems, like Dr. Phil. Isn't that wonderful? He'll be making plenty of money, too, I'm sure. Maybe even become famous and have his own talk show. There are so many doctor-type shows out there now. Everyone wants solutions to their problems."

Marissa could already see where this was headed. The mothers getting together, whispering about their children while making greeting cards or whatever craft project was on the docket. Mom confiding in Mrs. Newberry about her brokenhearted daughter in need of a quick love fix and the psychologist son who appeared to fit the bill. A dinner date was sure to follow the moment she stepped out of the car. "I don't think I'm ready for that right now, Mom. I mean, I haven't even gotten there yet."

"Ready for what? I just wanted to tell you there are others coming back to Cedar City the same time you are. You're not alone."

But Marissa was feeling very much alone at that moment. . . so alone that she wondered what could fill the void. Even if she was going back to what she knew first, with hometown streets and familiar names, old friends and her mom, nothing could claim to be the remedy. Though Mom was trying her best to stick a bandage on the wound.

"Well, thanks for the news." *I guess.*

"And the lemon bars will be waiting for you when you get here."

Marissa smiled. Mom remembered her craving for home-made lemon bars when she was a little girl. Oh, how she loved the mixture of sour and sweet the bars delivered in every bite. Maybe there was a lesson to be learned—that the sour things in life, tempered with the sweetness of God, could make things yummy in the end. And the thought of freshly baked lemon bars might be a good enough reason to return to Cedar City. "Thanks so much, Mom. That means a lot."

❧

Before leaving Omaha for good, Marissa decided on a visit to the cemetery one last time. She walked across the grass, past the marble blocks of stone in various shapes and sizes, until she came to Eric's grave. A smattering of grass seedlings had begun to turn the carpet of brown dirt into one of living green. "I'm leaving, Eric," she whispered. "I'm heading back to Cedar City. I know you'd want me to do this. . .to be happy and go on with my life." She twisted the engagement ring that stayed on her finger even during the months following his death. "Thanks for all the great times we had. For the way you loved me for who I am. But it's time for me to go. I can't keep looking at the past, and I know you'd understand that."

She tugged on the ring, allowing it to slip off her finger and into a zippered pocket inside her purse. This was it. She was saying good-bye to a part of her life forever. She would not look back but forward, with God's grace and mercy. It's all she could do.

Marissa turned to walk back to the car but stopped short. Another car, a huge white sedan, had pulled into the cemetery. She recognized it and the shape of the figure with a short, stylish hairdo and chic glasses sitting behind the wheel. Eric's mother. She inhaled a swift breath, thinking about the ring in her purse, wondering if she should slip it back on her finger for the woman's sake. Instead she hid her left hand behind her back as the woman got out of the car and headed toward her. Marissa always thought if they had been closer in age, Eric's mom might have become one of her good friends. She seemed so youthful in many ways. Vibrant and carefree. Different from her own mom. Only this woman had lost her beloved son. And now she appeared to have aged rapidly in the last few months.

"I thought you might be here, Marissa. I know you're about ready to leave town. I just wanted to give you a hug farewell."

"Thank you so much." She didn't quite know what else to say. Eric had always been the talker, bridging the gap between her and her pending mother-in-law. Mrs. Donaldson seemed to like her well enough. She frequently had both her and Eric over to the house for dinner. She was there the day Marissa tried on different wedding gowns. She helped Marissa pick out the place for the reception. She had ideas on a caterer, flowers, even a photographer. Eric said his mother was looking forward to having Marissa as her daughter-in-law.

"You're going to be just fine," his mother added, patting her arm. "You're a strong and beautiful young woman with so much ahead of you." She sighed, and Marissa saw the tears glimmering in the woman's eyes.

"I hope you don't think I'm abandoning Eric or the family by moving away," Marissa began.

Mrs. Donaldson stepped back as though surprised by the comment. Her gaze drifted across the cemetery. "Of course you're not. Eric's gone. He would want you to go on with your life. He always wanted you to be happy, you know. I only wish. . ." She paused, looking past Marissa in the direction of her son's grave. She shook her head. "Too many thoughts. So many memories, good and bad. It's hard. I only wish. . ."

"Only God can carry our losses, Mrs. Donaldson."

"Yes, you're right. He's strong enough to carry every burden." She seemed lost as she continued to stare at the grave site. She then looked back and managed a smile. "Now you take care of yourself. Where are you moving to again?"

"Cedar City, Utah. Remember, it's the place where I was born and where I grew up. I'm moving in with my mom temporarily." Marissa opened her purse and took out a small notepad and pen. "Here's my mom's address. I'll be staying there until I get a place of my own. And you have my cell number and e-mail address."

Eric's mother nodded, taking the slip of paper. "I should go back to Utah one of these days. It's been so long." She wiped a tear from her face. "Please keep in touch. Let us know how you are. I will always think of you as a daughter, you know."

Marissa and the woman embraced. She felt the dampness of the woman's tears across her cheek, the final living reminder of Eric. Marissa kissed her cheek and tasted the salty remains of the teardrops. "Good-bye and thank you for everything."

Marissa returned to her car, thinking of the ring in her purse. She opened the zippered pouch to see it there, safe. Mrs. Donaldson's car rolled along the narrow road of the cemetery, tires crunching gravel, and then headed into street. She wondered if the woman had noticed the ring missing from her finger. Not that it should matter. It was over. Would the memories fade with time as she embraced a new future?

Returning to the apartment, she gazed about the three bare rooms with boxes ready for the movers. Resting on the sofa was a photo album she had not yet packed away. Mom had put it together as a surprise gift one year. In it were memories of Cedar City and her childhood. There were photos of the downtown area. The walking trail into Cedar Canyon. A camping trip in Dixie National Forest with the youth group. And Bryce Canyon, where she went with the youth group on a retreat and where God spoke to her through the strange-looking rock formations called hoodoos. God was ready to set her feet on solid ground, or rather rock, as rocks were famous in Utah.

She made a mental reminder to return to Bryce one day for a visit. Maybe book a room at the lodge and wait for God to speak to her again. Ask Him what to do with her future now that the door had been shut to her hopes and dreams. Especially with Mom looking to arrange another relationship with the arrival of Wayne Newberry to town.

Marissa sank down on the sofa to look at the album once more. There were pictures of family at holiday time, including her dad before her parents' divorce when she was thirteen. Her older sister, Phyllis, who lived out in California. The family dachshund, Sunny, who died not long after Marissa moved to Omaha. She decided then she should think about getting another dachshund. They were such funny dogs, a veritable wiener doggie for sure. A puppy to train would certainly fill her days.

She turned the pages. There was a picture of her in the black evening gown she wore for the senior prom, standing beside her date, Wayne Newberry. Tall, dark-haired, a winning smile, a fine catch. She couldn't imagine him single. *Maybe he's divorced.* She shook her head, refusing to be mixed up in a situation like that, with some ex-wife in the picture.

She examined a few more pages. Pictures of college. Ski trips. And then a few of Eric with the blue eyes she adored. She traced the defining features of his square jaw and the lips she tasted many times, though it seemed like ages ago.

What should she do with such memories of Eric? Try to keep a semblance of them alive? Or take the pictures out of the album and surrender them, perhaps to Eric's family? They might like them, after all. For her, at times it was too painful still to even look at them.

But she couldn't let them go. Not yet. Eric was her life for a long time, ever since college. Even with the move, he would not simply vanish from her thoughts. Not with the memories of an engagement and sharing kisses on pleasant evenings, along with plans for a future and a family.

Marissa leaned back against the sofa. Eric was such a good kisser, too. He picked the most romantic places to sit and talk or share dinner over candlelight. He always remembered their engagement anniversary each month with a bunch of roses. She had so many glass vases, twelve of them to be exact, that she'd finally given them to Goodwill. He was a nice man, too nice to have his life shortened like that. But now he was enjoying heaven. He loved God, like she did. He was ready to enter eternity, even if God had called him to heaven sooner than anyone expected.

Marissa closed the scrapbook. She was ready now to close the book on this life in Omaha and open a new book and a new page. *God, I give this all to You. My move back to Cedar City. My life, my future. The future I once thought I had has changed so much. It wasn't the future You wanted me to have, I guess. So I ask You to please open the right doors for me and show me what to do with my life. In Jesus' name.*

She knew at that moment she was placing her destiny in God's capable hands.

❧

Marissa watched the movers carry out her boxes and furniture. This was really happening. Life was changing. Good-bye to the old. Hello to the new. Thankfully Mom had a friend who could keep her furniture until a future apartment became a reality. And Mom had made room in a large closet for the rest of Marissa's belongings.

The cell phone rang. "So are you really coming?"

"Of course I am, Mom. Why would you think I'm not?"

"I don't know. Maybe it was a bad dream I had last night. I woke up thinking you were married and staying in Nebraska for good. And worried that you might be blown away by one of those awful tornadoes. We don't get storms like that here. At least I never heard of one. We just have to watch out for forest fires. Thankfully I haven't heard of any yet this season."

Marissa wanted to tell Mom that she wished the dream had come true. She didn't want to move, after all. She loved Eric and wanted them married. But that was no longer the plan.

"Are you there, Marissa? Hello?"

"Yes, Mom, I'm still here, but I have to go. The movers are loading the van right now. I should be there in a few days. It takes time to get there. It's a long way."

"You were too far away, living in that place. Now at least one of my girls is coming home. Your sister won't, of course. She's staying in California. Oh, by the way, I'm having a party to welcome you."

Oh, no. Marissa sighed. A get-together filled with well-meaning guests was not something she wanted to endure right now. Peace and quiet seemed better remedies. Time to readjust and settle down. "You don't have to do that, Mom. In fact—"

"Don't worry, it's nothing big. Just some family friends and others you might know. You're going to be very surprised."

Marissa wondered if she would see friends from the youth group. Or the old high school days. Until she thought of Wayne. Mom would no doubt invite him if he was in town.

Marissa thanked her and hung up, just in time to instruct the movers to be careful with a chair that had a loose arm. She was glad at least for the "welcome home" sensation that flowed through the conversation. It sounded as if Mom couldn't wait. Marissa only hoped she could find a smile to plaster on her face. She wished she didn't have to pretend. There was still some heart mending to be done. If only it hadn't come to this. *But it has. And I will make the best of it, Lord, with Your help.*

two

"You're looking just great, Marissa."

He stood there wearing a smile, dressed in a sports jacket over a polo shirt, leaning against the frame of the door inside Mom's home. Wayne Newberry. He still had the wavy, dark brown hair she remembered from high school, but he now sported a mustache. He fit the bill of a successful doctor as if he were ready to embark on his own syndicated show. He had all the right everything, it seemed.

"Thank you." She managed to slip by him and to the refreshment table. As usual, Mom had outdone herself. It came from her work at the grocery store deli, where she got bargains on everything. There were ribs, tacos, cold salads, a relish tray, and, of course, a huge glass plate filled with her mom's famous lemon bars.

"I'm sure it must be difficult coming back here."

Marissa turned to see he'd followed her. For an instant, she scanned his left hand and saw no wedding band. She shook her head, hoping he hadn't seen her looking. Mom had already told her he was single. Not that she should think about such things. She'd only just arrived. She had boxes to unpack, a job to secure, people to reconnect with, her life to rearrange. And maybe a dachshund puppy to complete the picture, if she could talk Mom into the idea.

"Well, this is still home to me," she now said to Wayne and bit into a carrot. "And everyone has been really great. Did you know I got to see Denise for a little bit? You remember her from high school. She said Joy was here, too, but Joy's been sick. Come to find out, she's expecting."

She couldn't tell if Wayne was listening as he picked up a plate and selected some food from the buffet while she talked. Marissa looked around to see many of the guests giving her looks ranging from the curious to smiles to faces laced with sympathy. She knew they were probably considering her circumstances. What happened in Nebraska with her fiancé. Her move back here. And probably thanking God they were not in her shoes.

"How about going out for coffee sometime and catching up?" Wayne now asked.

She barely heard his invitation amid the thoughts cluttering her brain. "Huh?"

"Go out for coffee sometime?"

"Oh sure, that would be fine." She gave a small smile and then felt a tug on her arm. It was another of Mom's friends from her craft club, a Mrs. Carson.

"You look so thin and pale, Marissa. It's a good thing you came back to Cedar City. We'll have you looking healthy in no time."

"It's very nice to be back, Mrs. Carson," she said politely.

"Oh, come now, I know how it is. I lost Stanley a few years back. Remember that, Rosie?" She yelled at Mom above the noise of the guests.

"What was that?" Mom yelled back and then came over. The two had an open conversation over Mrs. Carson's husband, who'd passed away, and how long it took for her to recover. She then told Marissa how she cried every night and couldn't cook but resorted to eating those horrid frozen dinners and bags of store-bought cookies.

Marissa fanned herself with a napkin and wished she could

escape from all the chatter to the back deck for a bit of air.

"And I felt the same way when Ralph left me," Mom said, giving Marissa a look. "I was so lonely." A broad smile filled her face. "But no more!"

Marissa managed a smile. With everyone now engaged in conversation or occupied with the food, she slowly made her way to the back door that led to the deck. Opening it, she stepped out into the warm summer evening. The sun's fading rays had just begun to set fire to the red rocks and earth of the Utah landscape. She breathed in the strange air. How different this was from the hustle and bustle of Omaha.

She and Eric had taken a road trip to the western part of Nebraska once to see rock formations reminiscent of what existed here in Utah. That day she'd felt a longing for her native state. They stopped to tour the national monument called Scotts Bluff and the landmark of Chimney Rock that pioneers ventured past on their way westward along the Oregon Trail. It was all so interesting to her. Eric and she had a good time together, though he said he was glad to be back in Omaha. He liked trips on occasion, especially if it was to the ski slopes. But he preferred the closeness of people and neighborhoods with houses one after another, as if he found security in numbers and social networking.

Marissa walked onto the deck and down the steps to the backyard, where the grass was wilting from the intense heat. Mom must have forgotten to put the sprinkler on the last few days, which was the only way grass could survive the harsh Utah summers. She thought back to when she was little, playing in the backyard with Phyllis. Pretending to be a queen in a court. Playing with Barbie dolls. And then her teen years, of trips to canyons and ski trips in the rugged mountains. Of walks around town, sipping sodas and laughing. Now she was back to begin life anew. Or find out what her life should be now that it had taken a radical detour into the unknown.

After a while, a few guests began drifting out into the backyard to share a few sentiments with her. Others joined in, and the party moved outdoors. Mom threw on a switch, and an array of party lights in glowing colors, strung along the back railing, enlivened the atmosphere. Marissa sighed. Now was not the time for thoughtful contemplation. It was back to mingling and trying not to be a party pooper at her own party.

When the guests finally left, Marissa collapsed into the chair and flung away her flip-flops, glad to be off her aching feet. She was still buzzing from all the conversation and too many lemon bars. Mom pronounced the party a success and occupied the chair opposite Marissa, holding a steaming cup of coffee warmed in the microwave.

"Won't that keep you awake?" Marissa asked.

"It's decaf. You want some?"

Marissa shook her head and looked down to see food that had been dropped on the carpet.

"Did you have a good time? I saw you and Wayne talking."

"We chatted a little. He asked me out for coffee."

"Oh, how nice. I hope you said yes."

"We'll go eventually. I need to settle in, look for job and a dog, things like that."

Mom's eyebrows rose. "A dog! Heavens, Marissa, why do you want a dog?"

"Because I miss Sunny. I feel like she should be here. I was looking over pictures from that album you gave me. She was such a sweet dog."

"She was a nuisance. And dumb as they come."

"Mom!"

"I don't see how you'll have time for that. There are so many things to do here." She paused. "But I know you didn't come back here to have me tell you what to do. You're grown up, after all."

"Uh, yeah. Twenty-five, to be exact." Marissa added silently, *Too old to have my mom directing my life, but too young to be nearly a widow.* She couldn't exactly call herself a widow, as she and Eric hadn't exchanged wedding vows. But at times they had seemed to act as if they were married. For instance, a week before he died, Eric had put her name on his bank account and even gave her money. Why, she didn't know. He'd told her it was for a rainy day, to use when she needed it. That was like a husband in her mind, trusting her with his worldly possessions.

"Oh, I wanted to tell you. I have a friend who would be glad to hire you for her gift shop. This is the time of year when it gets busy, with visitors coming to Cedar City on their way to canyon country."

Work at a gift shop. Now wouldn't that be just the thing to reintroduce herself to the climate of Cedar City reeking with tourism. She nearly laughed but diverted her attention back to the crumbs sprinkled on the carpet. She stood and went to fetch the vacuum.

"I don't think I've had anyone clean my house in years," Mom mused, staring after her. "Thank you."

Marissa realized it had been a long time since she'd been back here. She had visited while on college breaks. But since her move to Omaha after college, she'd only been back twice. "It's been a while, but now I'm here. Let's tackle the dishes and get them out of the way."

"I'm too tired." Mom leaned back against the chair and closed her eyes.

Marissa headed for the kitchen, where she spent the next

hour washing dishes and cleaning up the refreshment table. She thought then of Wayne, piling his plate with food. And then his offer for coffee. Maybe she should try this new route and see where it led. "Hey Mom, do you have Wayne's phone number?"

"Hmm. Whose number?"

"Wayne Newberry's?"

"His mother's number is on the refrigerator door. I should remember it, but I can't even think right now. I'm so tired."

She didn't want to call his mother but dialed it anyway. After speaking to Mrs. Newberry, who gushed over how well Marissa looked and how happy Mom was to have her back, she obtained the number. "I just know Wayne will be tickled pink to hear from you," Mrs. Newberry added.

Wayne's deep voice answered when she called. "Marissa, this is a surprise. You okay?"

"Hey, I was wondering if that coffee invitation is still valid."

"Of course it is. I just asked you tonight. Want to make it tomorrow morning? Eight a.m.?"

"Okay. After tonight, I'm going to need a good latté to get me going."

He laughed. "There's a good coffee place in town called The Grind. Mom was telling me about it. I think it's new since we both moved away."

"Great! See you there." Marissa hung up the phone. Wayne Newberry. Old high school flame. Well, why not? Might as well see if any of the flame was still burning.

❧

Marissa arrived for her morning brew to find Wayne at a table with the newspaper spread out. He stood to his feet the instant she walked in and smiled. "What will you have?"

"Oh, you don't need to buy me coffee."

"Of course. That's why I suggested it. A latté, right?"

"An iced hazelnut latté and an apple cinnamon muffin would be great. Thanks." She took a seat opposite him to see the newspaper opened to the classifieds, and in particular, real estate. Wayne must be thinking of buying a house. Which reminded her that she should be looking for a place. She took up the paper and began scanning ads for apartments when he came back with her latté and large muffin on a plate. "Thank you. So are you looking to buy a home?"

"I'm thinking about it. Looks like there are some good deals."

"I need to find myself an apartment sometime in the future, once I get a good job lined up." She sipped the latté, strong but cold on her throat. "So what have you been doing since high school?"

He closed the paper and folded it in half. "I took off for college like most everyone else and lived away for a few years. I decided to come back here and set up my psychology practice. I deal with teen and college issues. Runaways, drug addiction, that kind of thing. Being a college town, there's plenty of that to go around. Not to make light of a problem. Too much pressure on kids these days. But it seemed like a good idea."

"It sounds like a good thing to do." She took another sip, sensing the latté would have her flying down the street with its potency. "I have to find a job. Mom says she can get me something to start in one of those downtown gift shops. Can you believe that's why I went to college. . .to work at a gift shop?" She grinned. "But it's better than nothing, I guess."

Wayne's face crinkled as he laughed. "My mother says we still get plenty of tourists on their way to Cedar Breaks and

Bryce. It's that time of year. First the tourists, then the college kids."

"I saw the RVs passing through when I arrived. The town pretty much looks the same. Still has the historic district, the nice parks—though the walkways are looking better."

"Not that many changes from what I've seen, and I've only been here a week myself." He finished his coffee, then stood to get a refill. Marissa took time to admire his tall, athletic build and broad shoulders. The wavy, dark hair and dark eyes. And large hands. Wayne had a lot going for him. She wondered why things didn't work out in the marriage department. She would love to ask but knew it was highly personal.

He returned to his seat opposite her. "I was very sorry to hear about your fiancé. How are you doing?"

"Well, what can one do after something so unexpected? But I'm doing better. I've had time to work through it. Everyone here's been great since I got back. I mean, the party Mom threw was nice. I think I made the right choice in leaving Omaha."

"Of course you did. This is home, and people care about you. When a crisis hits, most find comfort and security in the things they know and love."

"When I saw the red rocks and canyons and little trees, I thought, yes, this is where I grew up. This is where my friends and family are. It isn't where I went to college, of course. . ."

"You took off for Salt Lake or something, didn't you?"

"I went to Utah State, and that's where I met Eric. He was in one my classes, but we found out we both loved skiing. We spent a year on the ski team together. He taught me quite a bit. He was a year ahead of me and graduated, then moved back to his home state. But we stayed in contact through texting and the Internet. And phone calls, of course. He'd come to ski sometimes. Then he got a good job in Omaha, where his family lived, and asked if I'd be willing to move out there after graduation so we could be closer. I thought I was doing the right thing by moving there. Even if Mom wasn't happy with my decision to live out of state." Her voice trailed off as she sensed the doubt creeping in.

Why did she let such thoughts rise up? Like the idea she'd made a mistake by agreeing to marry Eric, which is why he died. It was foolish to even consider it. But she wondered, too, as Wayne sat looking at her, if he thought this was a perfect orchestration of events to bring them together after years of separation. "I wonder if sometimes I made the wrong decision. Marrying and living so far away."

"I know it's hard figuring out why things happen the way they do. I get people psychoanalyzing themselves all the time about their personal choices. Sometimes we have to make choices and see how they work out. And sometimes decisions lead to unhappy and even tragic results, and for no reason at all." He leaned closer, his coffee-colored eyes burrowing into her. "But you are *not* to think you did anything wrong here, Marissa. You followed your heart. And I'm sure you and Eric had a great time, even if it was brief."

"Yes. I'm glad for the time we had. He was a great guy." She sipped her latté. "Sorry I'm bringing all this up. I'm sure it's not what you wanted to hear."

He smiled. "I have no agendas. I just want to catch up with a friend from the old days and find out what's happening in her life."

"Well, now you know the nitty-gritty. And why aren't you married? A guy like you with a potentially successful and profitable career. Lots of women to choose from, I'm sure."

He lowered his gaze to stare at his coffee cup, and she wondered if she'd unintentionally hit a nerve. "It didn't work out for me."

"Oh, I'm sorry. Divorce?"

"No. I suppose it's good it ended when it did, or it might have turned out that way. We were all set to head down the aisle. Had wedding plans prepped and everything. Then Leslie got cold feet. She wasn't like you."

Marissa sucked in her breath, wondering what he meant.

"A levelheaded person," he finished. "Knowing what you wanted in life and going for it, even if it didn't always work out. Leslie had some nice traits, but she and I, we just didn't mix. Locked horns a lot. Argued. She had some problems left over from childhood."

"I guess it's good you didn't go through with anything, then."

"Marissa, I could never see you and me arguing. We seemed to hit it off real well in high school. I kind of wish now that we hadn't gone our separate ways when we graduated. Maybe things would have turned out differently."

"I don't know. Like you just said, Wayne, it makes no sense trying to dissect what we each did. But right now, I'm asking God what to do about my life. I hope you will give me the chance to do that. I. . .I'm not ready for anything right now."

His face reddened slightly. "Of course. I'm sorry if it sounded like I was hinting at something. I'm just glad to see you back and doing well, all things considered. But you always were a strong woman." His face softened as if appreciating that characteristic, among other things.

Marissa was glad the conversation had gone well up until this point. She decided now might be a good time to part ways. She thanked him for the coffee and left the shop, thinking about the conversation and the look in his eyes that conveyed a longing to embrace the past. Wayne and she had had good times together. But it was a long time ago, and they were different people. *God, it's too soon for dating or anything else. I don't even know what I'm doing right now. I need time. Please let others know I need to sort things out. Where to go and what to do.*

Marissa entered her car and drove the streets of Cedar City. Familiar sights began to come back to her. The storefronts of Main Street. Then the entrance to the canyon walk, where she parked on a side street and decided to go for a wander. Many times as a high school student, she had walked the gravel pathways with friends, laughing over a guy they liked or the next activity in the youth group. They talked about the festivals that hit the town or gawked at strange tourists carrying their cameras. She should call up Denise and Joy and have them rendezvous here for a reunion and catch up. Just like she had with Wayne. But everyone was busy with their lives.

Marissa walked the path, or rather took a stroll through a multitude of memories. She gazed at the rocky canyon and landscape dotted with sagebrush, allowing the pungent aroma to fill her. She was so absorbed by it all, she didn't notice the man walking opposite along the path until she nearly collided with something yellow and furry at her feet.

"Oh, please excuse me." She jumped back. "I nearly stepped on your dog's paw."

"No harm done. Likely Goldie would have leapt out of the way. Sit," he commanded the large golden retriever. The dog promptly obeyed.

Marissa smiled and petted the dog's furry head, thinking on her promise to buy herself a dachshund puppy when she had the chance. She stared down at the dog sitting so obediently, waiting on the next command from her master, when the man swiped off his sunglasses. She looked up, and suddenly the air left her. She felt cold all over.

It can't be!

The man's cheerful face evaporated. "Are you okay? Did Goldie do something? She's usually real gentle. I've never known her to scare even a flea, though she doesn't have any. I use the monthly spot treatment." He laughed.

Even the laugh! Her breath quickened. It had to be some kind of dream. Or a vision of her own making. Maybe even a hallucination. All she knew was. . .her beloved Eric was standing right before her very eyes!

"Are you all right?" he asked in concern. "Are you sick?"

"I. . .I. . ." She began to back away. "I. . .you look so familiar."

He laughed. "Wish I could say you did, too, but I'd be telling a tall tale." He chuckled again.

Oh, dear God, have You brought Eric back to life? Is this real? Did something strange happen? A miracle maybe? Or had he come back and now he had amnesia or something? "Is your name Eric?" she suddenly blurted out.

"What? No. I'm Anson." He held out his hand. She made a feeble attempt to grasp it before her hand fell away. "Have we met?"

"I—I'm sorry." She spun about and hurried away. When she turned back to look, the man was walking in the opposite direction. He then turned, too. Their gazes met. *Dear God, what am I going to do? It's like he's come back. Eric's alive! But. . . he's dead. We buried him.*

Didn't we?

three

Anson could not get the woman's stricken face out of his mind. He gripped Goldie's leash. It was like she'd seen a ghost. She'd asked if his name was Eric. He must look like someone she knew. Someone close to her heart. That was obvious. He walked the trail leading farther into the canyon, then turned. She remained where she was, still staring at him. Compassion stirred inside him. How he wanted to help. He should go back and reassure her that he was not who she thought he was. He broke into a brisk walk, hoping she wouldn't leave. Her feet shifted. Her hand swept her face. But she stayed where she was.

"Hi. I'm not sure, but you seem upset about something," Anson said gently as soon as he got within speaking distance. "Want to talk about it?"

"I—I just can't believe how much you look like. . ." She paused. "Have you. . .have you ever lived in Nebraska?"

"No. Never been there, actually. I spend too much time traveling this state for my job."

"Did you ever go skiing in Park City?"

"Of course, though I'm not very good at it. Am I being interrogated or something?" He meant it in a friendly way, but she took a step back as if his words had been a swipe.

Her face colored. If it were not for all the questions, he might have enjoyed studying her features more. She was certainly lovely to look at, with her long, dark brown hair and eyes to match. If only he could wipe away that strange look

28

on her face that spooked him even now.

"I guess I'm losing my mind. You see, I lost my fiancé a few months ago."

Goldie took that moment to lie down on the ground and take a rest. The woman seemed to breathe easier as if things were more relaxed. Silently he thanked his dog. "I'm very sorry to hear that."

"I mean, he died just a few weeks short of our wedding. In a car accident. I used to live here in Cedar City, back in my childhood. I decided to return after it all happened, to start over again. And now I can't believe I'm seeing things. Thinking you look like him or something."

"It happens. Don't worry about it. But rest assured—Cedar City is my home and not anywhere else. Except I did grow up in St. George. But I do get around to other places."

She straightened. "Like where?"

"I work for the National Park Service, so I travel to other parks in the region. But I come back here on my days off to take care of Goldie. She has to stay behind when I travel, and I hate leaving her here."

"I hope to get a dog," she blurted out. "I had a dachshund growing up. I simply love them."

"A wiener dog!" he exclaimed with a smile.

She gave a shaky smile in return. "They do look like little wieners. But I love dogs. Eric and I would have gotten one once we settled, I think. I never did ask him about that. He had a saltwater tank filled with exotic fish. Some were the size of my hand. He even had a few living coral and those strange-looking anemones." Her voice drifted off, lost in thought, until she centered her attention once more on him as if studying his face. "Have you ever been in an accident?"

"Look, you don't really think I'm your dead fiancé come

back to life," he hedged.

"No, of course not. It's silly. I—I thought I was over him is all. Guess I'm not if I'm seeing things."

"It takes time to get over something this tragic. You can't do it overnight. Or even in a few weeks, I know. I lost both my parents within a year of each other. My mom to cancer, my dad to diabetes and probably a broken heart. Dad never got over Mom's passing." His face colored when he realized maybe he shouldn't have used that comparison. Not that he wanted anything to happen to this pretty woman before him, like losing herself in a thick fog of grief.

"He's been gone over six months. I thought that was plenty of time. I even took off the engagement ring he gave me. But now maybe I'm going over the edge instead. Especially after this." She began sidestepping away. "I'm really sorry to have bothered you."

"It's no bother, really." Anson watched her walk away, trying her hardest not to look back at him again. Inwardly he sensed she wanted him to be her dead fiancé resurrected from the dead. And that fact saddened him. He remembered Dad mourning for Mom. Clutching her picture to his chest, weeping. Saying he didn't want to live anymore, that he wanted to be in heaven with her. At this, his feet began to shift. He wanted to dash back to that woman and tell her to live. Not to throw her life away. Or imagine him as the one she'd lost. She was young. She had so much of life ahead of her. And love, too. Things bright and sunny, not dark and dreary. *God, help this woman in her grief.*

When he arrived home, he immediately called his friend Carl to tell him about the events of the day. Carl would be glad for the encounter, as strange as it had turned out. He'd been on Anson to start looking into the dating scene. Anson had decided to irritate his friend and take his own sweet time. Until now.

"Interesting," Carl remarked when Anson told him of the abrupt meeting on the canyon walk.

"Is that all you can say? Interesting?"

"Well, it's an interesting way to meet. Not that I would want to look like someone's dead fiancé. Too bad. I've been saying a prayer for you, Anson. For a miracle. Not exactly the way I thought it would happen, though."

He frowned, even if his friend couldn't see his reaction. "Thanks a lot."

"The problem is you're never around town long enough to make things happen with a woman. Especially with the kind of work schedule you keep. Don't you leave for Cedar Breaks tomorrow?"

"Actually, I have a few days off. They switched my schedule around."

"So that means I don't have to take care of Goldie for a few more days. Yahoo!"

"Yeah, and I'm sure she'll miss you." He looked down at the golden retriever nestled at his feet, her furry head resting atop his tennis shoe like it was a pillow, dog drool staining the nylon.

"Everyone has their doubles walking around out there. I guess you were hers."

"Yeah. She asked all the questions, too. It was really strange. I wonder if she might need some help. A little grief counseling or something."

Carl chuckled. "She should have said you looked like a crown prince from Saudi Arabia. That would net you all kinds of attention."

"Yeah, a modern day *Prince and the Pauper* come to life. But she was pretty insistent. In fact, she asked me if I'd ever been to Nebraska. If I'd ever been in an accident. Things like that."

"Sad. You're right, it sounds like she could use some help."

"Yeah. Made me think of Dad when Mom died. I kind of wish now. . ." He hesitated. A lump formed in his throat, and he was unsure why.

"Don't go that route, Anson. You didn't do anything wrong."

Maybe God was putting his finger on something. That he still blamed himself for not seeing the warning signs in Dad. Of his depression. Not caring for himself, like the diabetes that eventually stole the man's life. The way Dad slipped away so fast. Anson should have watched over him better.

"Anson? Did you hang up? Hello out there."

"No. Just thinking."

"Bad thing to do sometimes."

"Yeah. It's not good to dwell on this anyway. It brings up things that should be gone. I need to read the Bible. I don't like what this is doing." He didn't want to elaborate on what still bothered him. Carl wouldn't understand it anyway. The only one who could was Lucy, his sister.

"Don't let it get to you. Think of the opportunities, instead. Like the attention of this lady." Carl went on, talking about the woman Anson had seen on the canyon walk. "Maybe it gives her comfort to know her fiancé will be resurrected one day. I mean, I once had someone who thought I was a dead ringer for a guy that played in a rock band. Now there's an interesting double to be. A Christian rock star who won a Dove award."

Goldie began pawing at Anson's leg, summoning him to dinner. "Look, gotta go, Carl. Thanks for everything."

"Not sure I did anything, but you're welcome. And about

the encounter? Don't worry about it. Just a knee-jerk reaction on her part. I'm sure you'll meet again, and it will go much better. And then you can ask her out."

Anson smirked and said good-bye. Rousing the dog from her comfortable position on the carpet, he went and poured kibble into a bowl for Goldie. He thought then of the woman and how she wanted a dog. Goldie had been a find at the city kennel. Dogs brought comfort when life dealt a bad deck. A dog would be just the ticket for her. Maybe he ought to offer to accompany her to the town kennel and look for a wiener dog. Or look for a dog on craigslist.

Goldie crunched down the dog food in less than two minutes, lifted her furry head, and looked at him with dark eyes.

"That's all you get, Goldie, or you'll get sick. You know it."

The dog cocked her head at him.

"Yeah, forget putting on the charm. So who do you think I look like? Perhaps a guy that a girl might one day want to meet?" He snickered. "Forget it. You don't have to answer that. I'd rather not know anyway." He stood before the mirror in the hall to see sandy-colored hair and a dark shade of blue to his eyes. Fairly tall, despite the fact that Mom said he was a preemie with health problems. He'd overcome whatever ailed him, even the asthma as a child. Mom would be proud of what he'd become and where life had led him, especially his faith in Christ. If only she hadn't died so early from cancer. Then Dad from uncontrolled diabetes. Anson swallowed the knot in his throat when he thought of it. Dad refusing to monitor his sugar. Anson asking him to go see the doctor when he began exhibiting strange symptoms. The man clinging to a picture of Mom with his gnarled fingers, wishing her back in the land of the living. Lucy finding him unconscious on the ground a week later. He died at the hospital. Yes, Anson had sympathy for the young woman he'd met today. Death of a loved one was difficult, especially one who was, or is to be, your life partner. Unfortunately, Anson wasn't sure he would ever see her again to offer his condolences. And maybe more.

&

Anson decided on another venture the following morning into Cedar Canyon. After yesterday's rather abrupt encounter, he and Goldie didn't get the kind of walk in God's good earth that they both needed and deserved. Usually they would do at least three miles, enjoying the scenery. Today was a new day, bright and sunny, as days usually were this time of year in Cedar City. All sun and little else.

He opened the car door for Goldie to jump out of the backseat. He hooked on her leash. "C'mon, girl. We're going to try that walk again." He yawned, wishing he'd gotten more sleep instead of thinking too much. Like about the young woman and her distraught face yesterday. Dad and Mom. And other things. Such as wondering when he might find that special someone in his life. He inhaled a deep breath, enjoying the scents of sagebrush in the warm sun and the serenity of the river flowing lazily by.

And then he saw her, standing in the same place as if she'd never moved. He checked his watch, realizing he'd been here the same time yesterday.

She stepped forward tentatively. "Hi."

"Well, hi. I didn't think I'd see you again so soon."

"Look, I had to come back to"—she paused, staring, and then focused her gaze on the ground—"to apologize for what happened yesterday. You. . .well, you do look a little like my fiancé, but you're not, of course. In fact, I can't believe

I quizzed you like I did." She shook her head. "I guess I'm having problems."

He moved forward in a gesture of understanding, then stopped as she moved back. "You don't have problems. You're in mourning."

"Huh? I shouldn't be after six months."

"My dad mourned for a year after my mom died. He never really got over it. There isn't a timetable on things like that."

She pushed back strands of her hair. "Okay. Well, again, I'm really sorry." She managed a small smile and backpedaled.

He wanted to offer to go on a walk, to ask more about what happened. But she looked as if she'd rather make her escape, despite his interest in getting to know her. Her long, dark hair whipped about in the breeze. She had a tall, perfect figure. When he was a bit of a distance away, he finally turned to see that she'd vanished. He sighed and looked down at Goldie, who paced back and forth as if reminding him of their three-mile jaunt. Time to let this go. He should center his thoughts on his upcoming work this week anyway in visitor relations—his area of expertise within the Park Service.

He frowned. So much for interacting with visitors and making them feel comfortable in their surroundings. Looks like he hadn't done too well in that area with the young woman. When problems arose with visitors or other situations that needed attention, he hoped for a calm and confident manner that would soothe a frazzled soul. Not so today.

He jogged the rest of the way back to the car, allowing his mind to go blank. He drove home, reaching it in a mere five minutes, just as his cell phone played a tune. It was his sister, Lucy. Must be God's timing, what with these memories of Dad and Mom, plus the encounter with the distraught woman. Lucy would know what to say and do. As he escorted Goldie into the house, he gave Lucy an abbreviated version of the encounter on the canyon walk.

He expected to hear her usual female inquiries and explanations, as only Lucy could do. "So she really said you looked like her fiancé?"

"Dead ringer, I guess. Oops, that didn't come out right. Sorry. I feel badly for her."

"Ever had anyone tell you that before, Anson?"

"Tell me what?"

"That you look like someone."

"Not that I remember. But she just lost her fiancé, so it makes sense. I can understand the reaction. I mean, remember Dad?"

"Yeah, I guess so." There was silence. Finally she said, "Hey, are you busy tonight? Got time to come over to my house for dinner? We haven't seen each other in a while. The boys would love to see you again. They miss you."

Something wasn't right in her voice, but he couldn't put his finger on it. "Luce, is everything okay? I don't know if I can take another troubled woman. Totally kidding," he said hurriedly. "I'm there for you, you know that."

She chuckled in bursts. "Of course. Sweet of you. But I'm fine. So. . .can you come?

"Am I known to turn down a home-cooked meal?"

"Good. Look, I need to run."

He heard nothing more, but the unspoken words were loud. Especially the silence after he mentioned Dad and Mom. He prayed something wasn't wrong. Then he thought how cancer can run in the family. He shook his head, running fingers through his hair. *Don't go that route, Anson. Don't read into anything, okay? Think about the great meat loaf she makes.*

You get to play with your nephews. Just go and be together as family.

God, she's the only family I have. Please don't let there be anything wrong.

≈

"Anson!" the boys screamed when he entered, bearing gifts. He never came to Lucy's house in St. George without gifts in hand, and his nephews knew it. He watched them take the bags and open them to reveal the latest Lego kits. "Cool, Anson! Thanks so much." He'd asked them long ago to call him by his first name. Uncle Anson just didn't make the cut for a worthy title. And the kids obliged.

Lucy stood in the kitchen doorway, a small smile on her face as she wiped her hands on a towel. "I'm making your favorite, little brother."

"Meat loaf and potatoes au gratin. I was hoping you would."

"You demand the best," she said with a smirk.

He came to her and bestowed a hug. Her body stiffened under the embrace, but he forced himself not to read into it. "Will Frank be here, or is he working late?"

"He'll be here. Meal's just about ready." She turned and headed into the kitchen to check on dinner. He followed, watching her. Something wasn't right. She couldn't look him in the eye. She stood hunched over and not because she was fixing the meal. A heavy burden lay on her shoulders.

God, what could it be? He decided to go gently. She would tell him eventually. "So is work going okay?"

"Oh, work is fine. Thanks." She shook her head as if to dismiss something else that had popped into her mind. How he wanted to know what lurked beneath her fine, raven black hair. They had always been open with each other. Especially after losing both Dad and Mom. They talked often. He about work and Lucy about family. Sometimes she confided in him about her and Frank, who could be a difficult man.

Just then the front door burst open to admit the burly man, who worked in postal delivery. Immediately the boys showed their father the kits Anson had given them.

"Nice."

Frank politely shook Anson's hand. They didn't share much in common, but Anson was pretty sure Frank loved his wife. Though right now, Anson couldn't be sure about anything.

Dinner was a quiet affair for the adults while the boys chattered away about school ending in a week and what they planned to do this summer. Frank asked about Anson's job and if he expected a good tourist season this year.

"Shouldn't be any different," he said, stirring cream into his coffee. "But I hope it will be another quiet summer." He looked over at Lucy, who had not spoken a word the entire meal. *Maybe she and Frank are having issues.*

Lucy jumped to her feet and began clearing the dishes from the table. "Let me do that, Luce," Anson told her. "You made a super dinner."

She managed a smile. "Glad you liked it."

"And I hope we're going to get a chance to talk."

She looked over at the clock and then her husband. "I don't know. It's getting kind of late, Anson, and you've got work, I know." Her eyes darted back and forth.

"I always have time for you."

She shrugged. "Yes, but. . .well."

"Can I at least talk to you? About relationships? Get a woman's perspective to help this lowly bachelor see things better?"

Her eyes grew large. "Oh, of course!" For once he saw her perk up, as if he'd offered some life-changing announcement.

He had none, of course, only that he wanted to know what was going on with her. But sitting there, he didn't know the words to say. She asked Frank to take the boys upstairs to play before leading the way to the sofa.

"I've been praying you'll find someone to settle down with, Anson. I mean, time is passing on. You're what, twenty-six?"

"Twenty-seven. Remember, you made me a big birthday cake with two and seven candles on it back in March. Had a great party. You even invited some of my ranger pals." He laughed, then grew quiet. "We're it as far as family goes, though. It's just you and me."

She grew quiet then. "I never thought we wouldn't have our parents. They will never see their grandkids grow up. I miss them a lot."

"I do, too. I guess the visit with the woman at the park made me think of them. Losing the ones you love. Dad never got over it." He paused. "Sometimes I want to blame myself, Luce, which I know isn't right. If I'd been more forceful with Dad when he wasn't feeling good. Got him to the doctor in time. . ."

"Anson, don't you dare blame yourself. Dad was a stubborn man. But he was more stubborn in handling his grief. Even if he wasn't accepting of your advice in the end, you brought a lot of joy to his life. To both of them. They never had any more kids, you know. Maybe Mom was having issues even then. I never did ask her. And then she died of ovarian cancer."

"Yeah." He hesitated. "Are you okay?"

Lucy straightened. "What do you mean?"

"Not sure, but you look like something's up. Trying to read a female mind, forget it. But you did seem rather distant tonight. I never knew you to go through an entire meal without talking."

She looked away for a moment. "Just trying to sort things

out. Looking for the right time for things."

"There is a time and a season for everything under the sun. Are you and Frank doing okay?"

"What? Yes, of course. Oh Anson, please don't try and figure everything out." She rested her hand on his arm. "I'm sorry if I look like I'm leading you on. We're fine here, really. I just wanted to see you again. We're all that's left in this family, like. . .like you said. Everyone else is gone. Though Dad's brother, Uncle Roy, might be alive somewhere. I'm not sure."

All this talk of family was good. A blessing. Something to cherish. He vowed to see her more often. To try and be there for her, despite what lay hidden. "Don't forget the Jamboree coming up soon."

"You know I wouldn't miss it. But you'd better be heading back. It's getting late."

He stood. "Take care, Luce."

"I'll tell the kids good-bye for you." She walked with him to the door, standing by his side like the older sister she'd always been. And a good sister, too. He didn't want to lose her. He spun around. "Luce, you don't have cancer or something, do you?"

Her eyes widened until they looked as if they might pop. "Anson! Whatever made you think that?"

"Just be sure you get yourself checked out. Cancer runs in the family. And I'll be sure to get checked, too."

She opened her mouth as if to say something, then nodded and answered with a simple, "Okay."

When the door closed behind him, the uneasiness still stirred within him. As much as he loved his sister, for the first time in his life, Lucy was like a stranger. And he didn't know why.

four

"I feel so silly and stupid," Marissa said, stirring the ice cubes floating in her iced latté. "I can't believe I walked up to a perfect stranger and asked if he was Eric. I must have been completely out of my mind." She took a long drink, hoping to find some solace in the man who was a doctor as well as a friend from long ago. Right now she needed both.

Maybe she ought to occupy the sofa in the corner of the coffee shop and confess all her woes of late, like the scene in a psychiatrist's office. The troubles seem to be piling up one on top of the other as each day played out.

"Maybe it's better it happened," Wayne said. "Now you're dealing with it. It's out in the open, so to speak."

She leaned over the table. "But I was so convinced for a moment it was him. He. . .he looked just like him. The same color hair. The blue eyes. The same build, well, actually this guy was taller."

"I hear that all the time. Everyone has a double walking around somewhere. Look at how many have sworn they've seen Elvis walking around. And now it's Michael Jackson. And other people. Like the people never died, which is unrealistic and unhealthy."

"Well, I don't care to make this the latest scoop in the *National Enquirer*, I'll tell you. I feel so dumb about it."

"It's going to be okay." Wayne smiled and gently took hold of her hand. "You'll be fine. Just let it go."

She craved his reassurance more than she realized. She'd

been so uncertain since that meeting at Cedar Canyon. She didn't know which way to turn or what to think. She was glad Wayne told her that seeing doubles was commonplace, but it still proved discomforting. Maybe because the feelings were still raw. As Anson pointed out, she hadn't truly recovered from Eric's death. She was still a basket case running around Cedar City, looking to find him alive in the people she met. Maybe it would take years and not months to get over this.

She glanced at her left hand, which Wayne still held in his, the hand that once displayed the brilliant diamond Eric had given her over a fancy dinner one night. She'd thought she'd said good-bye to it all that day in Omaha. She'd convinced herself it was time to move on. She believed she'd made the right decision by moving back here to Cedar City and starting over. Then why was she being plagued by another emotional storm?

Marissa shook her head and tried to forget it. She prayed with all her might she wouldn't see Anson again, as kind as he had been. She didn't think she could handle the emotional strain. She must bury it along with all the other unhappy memories.

"You need to do something for fun," Wayne suggested. "Take your mind off things. You know the Shakespearean festival is starting up. And I just happen to have two tickets." He released her hand and took the tickets out of his wallet, flashing them before her eyes. "I would love to have you accompany me."

"So they're still doing that every summer, huh?"

"Of course. It's Cedar City's trademark. Everyone's been talking about it. The hotels are starting to fill up. And of course, *Romeo and Juliet* is extremely popular. In fact, I think many of the shows are already sold out."

Marissa smiled, thinking how nice it would be to enjoy

a play and allow the moment to carry her away from the complexities of life. "I'd love to go."

His face brightened. "Great! Looking forward to it."

She was, too, as she sipped her cold latté. "Did you know that I did some acting in Omaha? We joined this little theater group. Eric said I had a knack for it. Of course when it came time for me to say my lines, I goofed them up. The other guy I acted opposite from was a professional, so he helped me. But Eric loved it." Her voice faded away to a whisper, realizing what she was doing. Allowing it all to drift to the surface. "There I go again."

"What?"

"Talking about Eric and everything. Sorry."

"Why are you apologizing? Of course you're going to talk about him, and probably for a long time. Memories serve as a way of accepting what's happened. Especially in the area of grief and loss."

"I thought I was having more problems by continuing to mention him like I do." *And running around Cedar City, looking for his double in strangers*, she chastised herself.

"Marissa, you can't pretend he never existed. That would be unhealthy. He was a big part of your life. Almost your other half. I'm sure you knew each other very well."

Marissa nodded before taking another long sip of her latté. Yes, she knew him. Everyone said they made the perfect couple. When she met him in college, they just clicked. She wanted to borrow his notes for chemistry one day after class. He was happy to oblige and came by with the pizza, too. From that moment on they were a couple. The relationship led them to his parents' hometown of Omaha where they both landed jobs and apartments after college. Wedding plans began in earnest until everything came crashing down that one awful afternoon.

Her thoughts flashed back to the guy she saw at Cedar Canyon and his similarity to Eric. Then she stared at Wayne. He was nice looking and not a bit like Eric. A dimple formed in the corner of his mouth when he displayed his wry grin. And he had dark hair and eyes. She told herself to stop dwelling on the past, Eric's double, or anyone else and concentrate on what the future may hold.

Now she watched Wayne take out his iPhone and show her the house he wanted to buy. As if it might yield some kind of exclamation from her. She hoped he wasn't expecting her to say something like, *I'd love to live in it, too!*

"It's very nice. But are you sure you want to live way up there in the hills? What will you do when it snows?"

"That's why I've got four-wheel drive. It seems like the perfect place to get away from it all. You can come see it with me later on this afternoon if you want. A woman's perspective on things would be nice to have."

"Well, maybe. I have to go job hunting."

Wayne looked at his phone. "And I have an appointment in the next half hour, so I need to run. Call me if you want to see the house." He stared for a minute, looking as if he wanted to kiss her good-bye. She flushed at the thought. Instead he pocketed his phone and headed for the door.

❧

I remember you saying how much a dog would help you right now. Maybe this would work. He practiced the lines in his head while staring for several moments at the screen, which displayed the pet listing on craigslist. Anson glanced over at the corner table, still using part of a newspaper to conceal his features while the woman he saw on the canyon walk pawed through her purse. He hoped to bless her by this announcement and maybe make things easier with regards to her loss. She took out a tube of lipstick. He thought of the man she had shared coffee with. He knew him. Or knew of him. Wayne Newberry. He and the woman had shared some deep conversation, though Anson couldn't hear the words. Occasionally her long finger would sweep a tear away from the corner of her eye. She then exclaimed over something Wayne showed her on his cell phone. He hoped it wasn't a dog as he looked at his own phone. He really should make his move now that Wayne had upped and left. He imagined Carl cheering him on, telling him to go for it.

Anson stood and moved to the table. The woman sat back with a start, nearly dropping her lipstick.

"Oh wow. I'm sorry, but every time. . . ," she began, then looked at her purse.

"I didn't mean to startle you. I was glad to see you here. There's something I found online that might interest you." She drew in a deep breath while smoothing back her hair. He gave her his phone. "See? There's someone right here in town who's selling dachshund puppies."

"You're kidding." She read the description out loud—eight-week-old puppies ready for homes. "The price is a bit steep, but for puppies, and miniature dachshunds at that. . .I have to see them." She searched for a pen to scribble down the information on a paper napkin.

"Actually, I already e-mailed them about the specifics." He took back the phone. "Here it is. 'We have two males and a female. I would like $150 cash each. They've had their first shots.' The owner is located on College Street if you want to stop by."

Marissa shot out of her chair. "I'm there." She then sat back down with a sheepish grin. "I suppose I'd better get some doggie stuff first. I don't have a thing. Food, collar, leash. A crate." She then slapped her forehead. "Mom. What will she think of all this?"

"Your mom?"

"I been living with her since coming back to Cedar City. She wasn't too keen on the idea of me getting a dog." She took out her phone. "I'll have to find out if the tide has changed." She placed the call while Anson forced himself to sit still and not fidget. "Guess she's at work at the deli. Wow, even though it will be a lot, this is something I need right now. We had a dachshund when I was growing up. A dachshund is the family trademark."

She sighed, looking so thoughtful and pretty just then, with her long, wavy hair. He was glad he'd been able to discover this. Maybe the tide was turning between them, too.

Anson cleared his throat, shoving any leftover nervousness he felt aside. "You know, we've met a few times, but you never did tell me your name."

"What? Oh, I'm sorry. It's Marissa. Marissa Jones. And you're Anson, right?"

"Right. Does your mom work at the grocery store here in town? I think I've met her a few times. They make a killer chicken that my pal Carl and I enjoy eating while watching the baseball game."

"Yes, Rosie Jones. I guess if you live here long enough, you get to know everyone. But I never met you until now, even though I grew up here."

"I grew up in St. George," he reminded her. "I didn't move here until after high school."

"That's right." She hesitated. "You know, I don't think I ever told Eric where my mom worked. I never talked much about my family. Maybe because I knew Mom wasn't thrilled about our engagement. I'm not sure."

Anson wondered about that and the apparent disagreements she'd had with her mother over things. He'd had a good relationship with his mom and was thankful for it until the cancer took her away. Maybe it was good Marissa was talking to a psychologist like Wayne Newberry. She could get the professional help needed to overcome these bumps in life. Like he wished he'd done for his dad after Mom died.

"Well, I'd better go find a job to pay for my dog," Marissa said. "And get some stuff for her, too."

"I take it you'll go for a girl."

"Of course. Girls have more fun." She blushed redder, looking even prettier than the finest rose. "Sorry, I didn't mean for it to come out that way. I meant that we girls have to stick together."

"If you say so."

"Anyway, thanks Eri. . .Boy, I almost called you Eric, too. This is crazy." She shook her head, managed an embarrassing grin, and headed out.

The aura of her presence still lingered, as did the pleasing aroma of her flowery perfume. Anson returned to his cup of now cold coffee, downing it before looking once more at the ad and picture of the puppies. Perfect. If only there wasn't the stigma of this Eric person hanging over everything. The mere fact sent a slight chill racing through him, despite the hot day. And sadness for her, that she still mourned so deeply. He checked the time on his cell phone, realizing he'd likewise better make tracks. He still needed to buy some chow for Goldie before he left town. Carl would be keeping her for four days while he roamed the Utah parks on business. And he'd better make sure he had enough food, as Carl had it in for him the last time the chow ran out, as did the dog biscuits.

Anson returned to his car and headed for the nearest big chain store and the pet department. Once inside the store, he stopped short. Standing in the aisle, perusing dog leashes and collars, was Marissa. He wanted to say something but instead ducked behind bags of dog food jutting from their places on the metal shelving in the other aisle.

"Can I help you?" a clerk asked her.

"Yes. I'm getting a miniature dachshund. I'm not sure what size collar I should get."

He watched as the clerk pointed out a selection of the smallest collars in stock. She held up several, checking the clasp and design before settling on a pink one. *Guess she's settled on a girl,* he thought. He admired Marissa's long fingers and her hair, which draped like a waterfall of molasses over her shoulders. Hardly any women he knew of wore their hair long. She then moved off to select a dog dish. Finally she tried to pull out a bag of puppy food, only to have several bags fall in an avalanche around her.

Anson immediately came over to her aisle. "You didn't hurt yourself, did you?"

"No. I guess they didn't stack the bags right." When she turned to face him, she gasped and stepped back. "Oh, it's you!"

"I know it looks strange, but I'm honestly not following you. I'd forgotten to get a bag of food for Goldie before I head out of town."

"I didn't think you were a stalker." Marissa smiled. "But guess what? I just talked to Mom, and she's agreed to have a go with the puppy. Reluctantly, with feet dragging, I think. But she's willing." She pushed back hair that had fallen forward. Suddenly she came out with a nervous chuckle. "Thank you so much for finding the dog. I still can't believe what I said to you out on the canyon walk. Talk about a major embarrassment. I mean, you really don't look anything like who I thought you were. I must have just been emotional and all, moving here. Too much to handle all at once."

"Well, a new puppy will surely keep you occupied. You won't be bored." She giggled at this, and excitement filled him. "Let me carry the bag of dog food to the checkout. I'll tell them to hold it for you until you've finished shopping."

"Okay, thanks." She smiled once more—a dazzling smile filled with perfect white teeth. She looked like a glamour girl in one of those commercials. She must be a model, he decided, but she didn't have that kind of outward personality. Still, she was warming up nicely to him. No longer did she stare at the ground or the sky above but looked him straight in the eye as if she were used to seeing him. Things were definitely starting to look up.

He strode up to the cashier and presented the dog food. In an afterthought, he went ahead and purchased it.

A few minutes later, Marissa hurried up, out of breath, to unload the other doggie goodies on the counter. "Oh, and the puppy food is mine, too. I still need to pay for it."

"It's been paid for already," the clerk said.

She stepped back. "What?"

"Welcome to Cedar City," Anson said quickly, managing a small smile before taking up his own bag of dog food and heading out the door.

He stopped to peek in the corner of the shop window and saw her standing at the checkout. She fumbled in her purse for her debit card, appearing quite flustered. She glanced around as if expecting him to still be there. He inhaled a sharp breath, wondering what she was thinking. How he wished he could read her thoughts. Did she like what he did? And consequently, did she now like him? When he saw her load the bags into the cart in preparation to leave, he moved quickly to his car. He must let it go for now. There was work to accomplish this week. But when he returned, he hoped their paths would cross again.

と

Marissa decided she'd had enough interesting encounters for one day and headed for home, leaving the puppy for tomorrow's adventure. She could barely breathe let alone think after what happened at the store. She thought of the dog food in the trunk, purchased by Eric's double, then shook her head. She mustn't think of Anson that way. True he did have a few similarities to Eric. But he was his own man, as Eric had been. And now she wished she'd said something different in the store. To stop with the apologies and move on as if nothing had happened. Even small talk about the weather would have been better.

She barged into the house and dumped the dog items in the foyer.

Mom hurried out of the kitchen. "What are you doing with all that?"

"Remember, Mom? I'm getting a dog. I don't have it yet, but. . ."

"Oh. I hoped you were joking when you mentioned it."

"What?" *Oh please, Mom. Don't do this to me.*

"I don't know if I want a dog here, Marissa, now that I've been thinking about it. While you were away at college and Phyllis was doing her thing, I had to take care of your dog. And she was so sick. It was awful. Especially when I had to have her put down."

"Mom, I know you did so much for Sunny. And I never thanked you for it. But really, it won't be like that. This is just for a few weeks until I can get an apartment."

Mom looked at her but said nothing.

"I don't want to sound desperate, but I really need this in my life right now, especially after everything that's happened." Marissa didn't spill the rest. . .that life was spinning out of control, despite her best efforts. Having the puppy—caring for it, training it, walking it—would give her something to shower love and attention upon. Something to rid her mind of Eric, Eric's double wandering around town, and Wayne's fingers caressing hers along with that look of interest in his eyes.

Mom stared at her for a moment, shook her head, and returned to the kitchen. Marissa looked at the dog food, thinking about Anson's kind gesture. She so wanted a dog back in Omaha but never broached the subject with Eric. He loved his tropical fish. Did Anson like tropical fish, too? *Oh, honestly, Marissa. Stop with the comparisons.*

"Marissa, I don't see why you need a dog now with everything else going on. You're just getting settled." Mom had reentered the foyer to look once more at the dog bowl, leash, and food.

"That's all I want to do is settle in, Mom. But it's hard. People here have been great. I've liked getting together with Wayne. I haven't been able to connect with others like I wanted, such as Denise and Joy from high school. Joy's been having morning sickness, and Denise is busy with her work. Maybe if I can reconnect with the church, though they have a new pastor. . ." Her voice faced away.

Suddenly Mom had an arm around her, giving a gentle squeeze. Marissa soaked in the comfort that eased the misgivings. She wanted to blurt out all the things going on inside but held back. "I know it must be hard," Mom said. "Give yourself time. And I brought home the ingredients to make you lemon bars. They always seem to cheer you up."

Marissa heaved a sigh. "Mom. . .what about the dog?"

"Look, I'm just glad to have you home. If you need the dog so much, okay. But he's your responsibility." Mom released her hold and said nothing more.

Marissa silently thanked God for this small miracle, one of many she needed in her life. She was doing things she never thought she would do a few months ago. Like returning to Cedar City when she thought she would be married and living a blissful existence in Omaha. She prayed that peace and purpose would reign in her heart again, even if both seemed absent right now.

five

"So who is she, Anson? Let's have all the juicy details. Please!"

Anson was busy scribbling notes, barely hearing the words of the young female ranger manning the information counter inside the visitor center at Cedar Breaks National Monument. "Who or what are you talking about?" he wondered absently. He was on duty as usual, ready to hear all the complaints and situations involving visitors—like trespassing, damaging park property and protected sanctuaries, people sick or injured or unhappy with the park in general. And he would smooth it over with conventional wisdom and sneak in some godly attributes as well. Like turning the other cheek to an irate visitor. Give good for evil. Deal in justice and the law. Say a kind and encouraging word—things that would soothe a distressed soul. And he'd already done that with a woman who said the park had injured her ankle. He'd smoothed it over with a sympathetic phone call and avoided legal action.

But now his fellow rangers were hammering him today, and he didn't know why. Did his face give away a telltale sign to the two women that something was going on? Like lines of tension running across his forehead or a certain look in his eye or maybe the pen trembling in his fingers. He thought he appeared rather composed, even if his insides were slowly twisting into knots.

"C'mon, I can see it. I actually heard you whistling as you work. Didn't you, Mira?" Sandy elbowed her naturalist friend.

"Yep, Anson was whistling all right. Some oldies song like 'Love Me Tender.'"

He peered up at the two young women who eyed him in anticipation while leaning forward, poised to hear any titillating gossip. "You two sure are nosy."

"C'mon, Anson." Sandy cupped her face with her hands, blinking her lashes rapidly. "We want to hear every detail."

He dismissed their interest to collect his notes, which took up the end of the information desk. A visitor bumped into him then and inquired about hiking trails in the park. Sandy let go of her curiosity to answer the visitor's question, while Anson took the opportunity to write a few more choppy sentences about his phone call earlier to the injured visitor. Thankfully the call had gone well, with the husband apologizing for making a scene and confessing they'd both been on the wrong side of the railing when the log fell on his wife's foot. If only all things could be this easy. He sighed in relief, thankful the situation had been resolved. Yet other situations loomed, ones he had little skill or knowledge in solving.

The visitor moved to the front door, and once more Sandy's attention was focused on him. "Mira and I had been taking bets when you'll find someone to date. So how about it? Who's right and who's wrong?"

"Ladies, you have entirely too much time on your hands. Maybe I should find some work for you to do." He chuckled while stowing away the papers.

"You're a great guy, Anson," said Sandy. "If I wasn't already going out with someone, you'd be on my short list." She laughed. "You should at least have a few prospects."

"Thanks for the interest, but it will happen when it's supposed to happen." Like everything else in life, he decided. But right now things were happening that he wondered if they were of God or not. Like the encounter with Marissa Jones that ended up hitting his heart and soul in an unexpected way. He had to admit, after the various encounters, from the canyon walk to the pet store, he had a distinct desire to know more about her. Like where she lived, for example. Maybe it was close by since she frequented the canyon walk. If she did live in the neighborhood, that would surely mean more encounters. And maybe friendly conversation would occur now that she was over the initial shock of their first meeting. They'd gotten the kinks out, so to speak. Hopefully she would deal with her grief and move on. They could enjoy walks with their dogs once she had her little Fido trained. Talk about their interests. Maybe it would lead to lunch, like a sandwich and coffee. Or dessert. Lucy loved desserts. Women liked chocolate, too, right? Marissa liked that shop, The Grind. And he would like to be the guy on the other side of the table rather than the psychologist, Wayne Newberry, who seemed a bit too friendly during their last encounter, in Anson's opinion.

"See, he's turning red, Mira," Sandy noted. "Anson, you're driving us crazy with all this secrecy!"

"Okay. Here's a little story for you."

The two women leaned over the counter, eager to hear every detail.

"I ran into a woman on the canyon walk in Cedar City who thought I was her dead fiancé come back to life." He expected laugher or looks of wonder. Maybe even sympathy.

Sandy's smiling face disintegrated into a look of bewilderment. "Are you joking or something?"

"Did you see something on a crime drama?" Mira asked.

"That's what happened. In fact she even asked me if I was him, if I lived in the same state as this fiancé and everything."

"You're kidding. You've got some crazy girl chasing after

you?" Now both women looked at him with wide eyes.

"No, nothing like that. She's very nice. She's just been through a lot. Her fiancé died a while back, and she moved here to be with family and friends. Of course, after a few more meetings, she decided I didn't quite look like him after all.

Sandy shook her head. "Maybe you are her dead fiancé come back to life, Anson. I saw that once on TV. Can't remember where. But the guy had amnesia and didn't know who he was."

He saw them both looking him over, wondering if he'd been smacked on the head. "I assure you I don't have amnesia. I still remember who you both are. Kind of." He grinned.

"Do you like her?" Mira asked.

Anson thought on that. "Yes, as a matter of fact, I do."

The women shrugged. "Well, I'd say you'd better go easy, then. Treat her with some of that mercy heart you give the visitors, Anson. You can't go wrong."

Anson thought it a good idea as he moved toward the door of the visitor center. Still he was embarrassed he'd spilled the beans about the whole "double" scenario. He should have respected Marissa's privacy. But the rangers were hungry for details, and he'd given them plenty to chew on.

He slipped outside and behind the visitor center to a clearing that overlooked the famous vista of Cedar Breaks—a huge bowl-like configuration with rocky formations colored like a mixture of table salt and cayenne pepper. In the distance other visitors gathered along the walkway to take in the beauty. The only thing that spoiled the scene were the dead spruce lining the canyon rim. The lifeless trees, damaged by beetles, stood out in sharp contrast to the colorful canyon. How like life. Beauty that could be easily marred by memories of those who had passed on, or other tragedies and loneliness. He would like to see Marissa stay beautiful. To not let what happened in the past ruin her like the scene before him. He should do as Mira and Sandy suggested—sprinkle mercy and kindness as the necessary ingredients for life and peace.

He returned to his SUV and tried setting his mind on his work. His next stop was the forest service center at Dixie National Forest. But his thoughts continued to drift. He should have another talk with Carl. Watch some sports and eat chicken. Then talk about women. Carl had a girlfriend. Maybe he should get Carl's take on how to approach a woman who'd been engaged. How does he get her to see him with new eyes and not with eyes that only saw her late fiancé?

❧

Anson thought over the game plan. He had it in the bag as far as Carl was concerned. Good food and sports go together. And so, too, would a talk about women. When he pulled into the grocery store, another thought occurred to him. Marissa's mother worked in the deli. It would be good to find out a little more about her through the mother. He knew Rosie by face. She was a model of perfection when it came to handling the deli, running it better than any drill sergeant could train the troops. Other than that he didn't know much else about her.

He strode into the busy supermarket and headed for the deli area. He didn't see the older lady. Instead some young woman who snapped her gum asked what he wanted waited on him. "Is Mrs. Jones working?"

"She left early."

Great. Anson sighed. So much for that. "Okay, thanks." Now the aroma of fried chicken tugged at him. He set to work assembling the meal—a box of chicken and potato salad to go along with it. He then meandered over to the bakery for an apple pie. Carl would never say no to this. And neither could he as his stomach churned with the thought of food.

Suddenly he spied an older woman wearing a store apron, ready to exit the store. He left the food sitting in a basket on the counter and ran out to intercept her. "Mrs. Jones!"

She whirled in surprise. "My goodness. Did I leave something in the store?"

"No. I'm sorry. I'm Anson McGruder. I often stop at the deli counter."

"Well, you're one of a hundred each week, I'm afraid."

"I was. . .I was wondering about Marissa."

The woman's eyebrows rose. "Are you a friend of Marissa's from high school?"

"Uh. . .well, we've met. . . ," he began. "On the canyon walk."

"Isn't it wonderful how she's come back to town? I'm so thrilled to have her back."

"I imagine you are. Any mother would be."

"I just hope I won't be in competition with her dog. She got herself a dog, you see."

"Really." So she did finally get the dog he'd suggested. The fact warmed him. He now had a connection with Marissa. "Well, I know it must have been tough on Marissa, losing her fiancé. I mean, when I first saw her on the canyon walk, she thought I was him."

At this the woman's eyebrows rose even higher. "Oh my goodness. I had no idea she was taking it so hard. I guess I should have figured it. Probably a good thing she and Wayne are seeing each other. Do you know Wayne Newberry?"

He nodded but was struck by the words. *Wayne and Marissa*

are seeing each other? He sputtered, "You mean he sees her as a client?"

"Oh, no. I just talked to Wayne's mother. Something is happening between them. They're going on a date to see *Romeo and Juliet*. He's quite a successful psychologist. And he's in the middle of buying a house, which means he plans to stay in the area. I think they're perfect for each other."

All the anticipation within Anson suddenly vanished. He shifted his feet. "That's nice," he said weakly, knowing full well he didn't mean it.

"Yes, well I'll have to tell her I ran into another one of her friends. She's looking to reconnect with old friends here in town, but they all seem so busy."

"Tell her I'll be walking my dog on the canyon walk tomorrow morning at eight. We can. . .we can talk about old times." Like times in the last few days, he mused. And maybe tell each other good-bye, too, now that Wayne Newberry had arrived on the scene and whisked her away. Anson wished he could probe more—how serious Marissa and Wayne were, and if that house meant she and Wayne were planning to marry in the future. If that were so, what about all that supposed grief she exhibited? Maybe it wasn't as bad as he thought. She must have overcome the melancholy quickly if she and Wayne were on some fast track to the altar. He stood there wondering if he had just wasted the last few days on some whim. *You should have never thought of her in any other way than a stranger you met on the canyon walk. Let it go and stop being selfish. Be glad she's finding a reason to go on.* But he wanted to be that reason.

Anson trudged back inside the store to find his basket of food long gone—disposed of by another gum-snapping clerk, no doubt. He went around picking out his dinner once again, hoping Carl was free tonight. He really needed to talk things over with him. Tell him the big news of the day—that love had once more eluded him, swept away by a psychologist's mind and heart.

☙

Over a plate of fried chicken accompanied by potato salad later that evening, Anson dropped the bomb. "Hey Carl, I just thought I'd let you know that, once again, love has sent me heading into another dumpster."

His friend never missed a beat when it came to food, but Carl surely missed the seriousness of Anson's news as he ate. "Well, I'm sure we all feel that way from time to time. Like we've been in the garbage heap of life." He dished up another huge helping of potato salad.

"I mean it."

Carl shoveled down a forkful of salad followed by a swig of cold soda. "Okay, so what's the deal? Where are you going with this? Because I've never known you to take a dive in the trash before." He chuckled and tipped back his chair.

Anson unfolded the details of the last few days and how Marissa appeared to have been seduced by a psychologist who sympathized with her woes. Carl said nothing, but in the middle of the story, his chair hit the floor with a thud. "Well, sorry to hear that, bud. I must say I'm really surprised how this woman has gotten to you. First time I've not seen you head over heels for your work in the Park Service."

"I know when we first met, she was shaken up. Thinking I was her fiancé come back to life or something. Then I thought I was starting to bridge a connection. Finding her the puppy. Buying the dog food. Now this guy comes out of nowhere and takes her away."

"You don't really know what kind of relationship Marissa and this psychologist have. It's hearsay from some overly eager and protective mother who wants things prearranged. Go do a few things with Marissa and see what happens. Like the walks you do in the canyon. Or take her on a road trip to one of your parks." He grabbed a dinner roll and reached for the butter. "We can even do a double date if you think that would help."

He thought silently on it, trying to imagine Marissa on a dinner date, her long hair reflecting in the candlelight along with her inquisitive eyes. Reminiscing over him finding the puppy for her on craigslist. He must still have a connection to her somehow, even with Wayne in the picture. There had to be something to grab hold of, no matter how small it was. "I'll try the walk first and see where things stand. If I can at least determine Marissa's intentions, I can take it from there."

Carl chewed, swallowed, then reached for his drink again. "Do what you want. Just keep your feelings and hers in check. If it goes south, get out fast. Don't wreck your lives over something that may not work out. But I wouldn't worry. You're good at interpersonal relationship skills, Anson. It's why they made you one of the chiefs in the visitor relations department. You're the genuine smooth talker in the area of visitor problems. So use your best skills to your advantage."

"I never thought I'd be solving my own problems."

"Anyway, speaking of your work in visitor relations, when do I get Goldie next?"

As if on cue, the huge golden retriever lumbered over and stretched out beneath the table at their feet. "Seven fifteen Wednesday morning. I head for Zion as soon as I drop her off."

"Okay. You hear that, Goldilocks? It's you and me again. And you'd better be good."

"Goldilocks? Look, Goldie is as good as gold. Hence the name."

"Sure, sure." Carl wiped his mouth once more on his napkin, then wadded it into a ball and pitched it unsuccessfully toward a nearby wastebasket. He stood to his near six-foot frame. "Well, thanks for dinner. Keep in touch, okay? I'd sure like to know how this turns out."

"Thanks."

Anson saw his friend to the door then moseyed on over to the living room and sank into a chair. Goldie followed suit and lay down at his feet. Just then a thought occurred to him. He stood and accidentally stepped on Goldie's paw. She let out a yelp. "Oops, sorry girl."

He went to his office and turned on his laptop. Once on the Internet, he typed Marissa's full name in the search engine. Several entries popped up, including a listing in a graduating class from Utah State. He perked up at this, recalling that she'd said something about skiing and clicked on the college ski teams. There he found Marissa Jones with her long hair flowing out of a knit ski cap. She wore a bright smile framed by flaming checks, holding a pair of skis upright beside her. She appeared quite attractive in the photo, like a model for a skiing magazine. He then looked over the faces of her teammates. No Eric was listed. Still, he was curious about the man who had nearly married her. What kind of man was he that had captured her heart?

Anson continued looking via the search engine. A news article popped up with Marissa's name in it. The article described the accident that killed Eric Donaldson. Anson bent to ruffle Goldie's fur as he read the difficult story and then the obituary that followed.

Eric Donaldson, 26, of Omaha, Nebraska, died December 3rd as a result of a traffic accident. He was born February

*28th in Park City, Utah, to Henrietta Clay (now Mrs.
Eugene Donaldson) of Omaha, Nebraska. He graduated
from Westside High School in Omaha and Utah State in
Park City, Utah, where he majored in computer science.*

*Eric was a skilled skier and an active member of the
Covenant Church in Omaha. He enjoyed being with family
and friends and lived life to the fullest.*

*He is survived by his parents, Henrietta and Eugene
Donaldson; a brother, Mark; his maternal grandparents;
aunts; uncles; cousins; and his beloved fiancée, Marissa Jones;
who will miss him dearly. He was preceded in death by his
paternal grandparents.*

*A Celebration of Life and Reception will be held Friday,
4 p.m.–7 p.m. at the Covenant Church. Private interment.*

He wished there was more about Marissa besides the few
photos from college and the simple yet profound statement
in the obituary. "Well, Goldie ol' girl, maybe I should take my
own advice and let this go. I've got things to do anyway. And
it doesn't make much sense worrying about it."

Just then the cell phone played a tune, disturbing his
thoughts. Lucy.

"Hi, Anson. I was wondering. . .well, how you're doing and
all."

"Doing good. You caught me reading an obituary, actually."

"What! Who died?"

"You remember me telling you about that woman on the
canyon walk who thought I looked like her dead fiancé. Well,
I was reading about the guy. And I can say that this fiancé
and I have nothing in common, which is good news."

"I. . .I don't understand. Why are you doing a comparison?
For what purpose?"

How could he confess that he was being nosy, that he liked Marissa and was hoping to find out what kind of guy she liked before someone else, namely Wayne the psychologist, stole her forever under the guise of some mental diagnosis? "I don't know. I just wanted to learn more about the man Marissa nearly married. Aren't you happy that I'm looking into the relationship department?"

"I don't know. Not like this."

He looked at his phone in puzzlement. He thought for sure Lucy would be happy he was attracted to Marissa. But maybe not. "She seems very interesting."

"She sounds like she has problems. Be careful. Anyway, I wanted to let you know that we're coming up for the Jamboree in a week. Will we see you, I hope? The kids are counting on it."

"Of course. Tell my nephews I'm taking them on the midway. And to see the old cars. Maybe I'll throw in popcorn and cotton candy for good measure."

"They will love it, I'm sure." She paused. "By the way, what did the obituary say?"

"Not much. The guy was originally from Park City. I know he and Marissa met in college. He was big skier. Computer guy. Stuff like that."

"Okay. Anyway, I'll see you in a week."

When the call ended he still stared at his phone, wondering what could be plaguing Lucy. Why was she so against Marissa? Was God trying to say something, but he wasn't interested in listening? Was he setting himself up for a big fall if he proceeded outside of God's will? *God, I know You will work this out if it's meant to be.*

six

The next morning Anson was treated to a pleasant sunrise, and he prayed, perhaps a new dawn in his life. He took Goldie out early to make certain she had a good walk before delivering her to Carl's. The sky was a perfect blue, as was normal for summer days in Utah. It felt quite warm but not humid. He had to admit, he was glad this was the day the Lord had made. That he would be making tracks for Zion. Visitor problems surely awaited him, but he could also enjoy the splendid scenery, like venturing into The Narrows—a popular walk within a canyon by way of the river.

He took out his phone and checked the calendar. Next weekend was the annual Jamboree, and he made a notation to contact Pastor Ray about helping at the church booth. Maybe he could take Pastor Ray aside then and discuss the issue of relationships. It might be good to have a man of God's take on these things and to keep him accountable in all areas of his life.

Anson began jogging along the walkway with Goldie when he saw a woman approaching in the opposite direction. The dog she handled was so small it could have fit in the palm of his hand. He skidded to a stop. "Now that is one tiny pup."

She stopped also, and suddenly he realized it was Marissa. Maybe the dawn was indeed rising, as he'd hoped. At first she appeared startled to see him, then relaxed. "Well hi, Anson. You're out early this morning. Meet my new boy, Sammy. The one you found for me *and* bought the food for. Which

I haven't been able to thank you for until now."

"My pleasure. So its Sammy, is it? I thought you might be getting a girl instead. You mentioned it when we talked about it at the coffee shop. What happened to the pink collar you bought?"

Her face pinked up, like the collar. "Oh that. I exchanged it for another. The lady just had male puppies left by the time I got there. Which is fine. Sammy, meet your uncle Anson. He's the one who found you. I owe him big-time, on several fronts."

Anson found the comment endearing. He liked it that he and Marissa were already speaking in terms of a relationship, even if that relationship was a simple one through their pets. "And Sammy, this is Goldie."

"Careful. Goldie's just a tad bit bigger than Sammy. More like Goliath meeting David." She laughed. He liked the sound, bubbly and bright like the sunny morning. She appeared more comfortable this time than in previous encounters. Maybe finding a dog and buying a bag of kibble did wonders with the dog owner, and a very attractive dog owner at that. "Don't worry. Goldie likes dogs, large or small." Goldie took the opportunity to nuzzle the pup. "See? Maternal instinct. Bet if you give them time, Goldie will have that pup under her wing. Or paw." He looked at his cell. "But unfortunately I have to run, so I can't see how the friendship materializes."

"Late for work?"

"I have to be in Zion by noon. And inevitably I'll end up behind an RV going twenty miles an hour on the highway."

"What do you do there? Are you a ranger?"

"Not quite. I'm in the visitor relations department. I make sure everyone visiting the parks is happy and fairly healthy.

Always something to be done. I'm responsible for several of the parks here. Cedar Breaks and Bryce, mainly. Sometimes I help in the national forest also. Zion, too, if they're looking for a second opinion, like today."

He saw her straighten. "Did you say you work at Bryce? I love that place."

"Maybe we could go there sometime." He knew he'd hit the bull's-eye when he saw her face light up as if a sunbeam fell directly on it. She stood still, pondering it all and, he hoped, him also in the equation. "Anyway, I'd better get going." Though inwardly he wished he had another hour. Or two. Or three.

"Okay."

Hope surged within him and set to rest, at least temporarily, any doubts raised earlier. Then she flashed him a smile, and nothing but her face appeared. He would have asked her right there about a future dinner date, except she'd moved off down the path. At least he had made inroads with the mention of Bryce Canyon. *There's always tomorrow. Or at least the day when I return from work.*

❧

Marissa took stock of the last few meetings she'd had with Anson. *Let's see now. He likes dogs. He likes Bryce Canyon; or rather he has connections to the canyon. He is adventuresome. He does look somewhat like Eric.* But the more she observed Anson, except for his hair and eyes, the more different he appeared. His build, for instance. He was taller, maybe, and thinner. Then of course there were personality differences. Likes and dislikes. She halted. What were Anson's likes and dislikes? She didn't know. Nor did she really know anything about him, save a bit about his job description and his dog. Not like Eric, whom she knew inside and out. Maybe it was time to discover someone new. And Anson was proving to be new and different. Especially with his love for the canine companions, which spurred her interest. Like the encounter this morning. She stopped again, even as Sammy tugged on his tiny leash and whimpered. "What if he lives near here, Sammy?" She hurried then to the parking lot but found him nowhere in sight. Hopefully they would see each other more on the canyon walk. Talk more. And find out things about each other.

Sammy whined again. Marissa scooped the tired pup into her arms and cuddled him. "I'll get you home, Sammy. Though it would've been nice to know where he lives, I must admit. Then we'd likely see each other more." She trudged back down the road to her mother's house where Mom stood watering the flowers. The harsh Utah sun baked everything in sight. Green lawns were only had by those who watered faithfully, and Mom was one who cared about having a green lawn and flowers. She liked color, and so did Marissa.

"Don't let that dog go doo-doo on my nice lawn," Mom warned.

"He did his business on our walk. I'm training him as quickly as I can so he isn't any trouble. And he's doing pretty good."

Mom said nothing more. At least she appeared accepting of the new addition, even if reservations remained. Marissa hoped it would go better in the days to come. Heading inside to give Sammy some water and then tuck him in his crate, she again thought about the encounter today. One particular tidbit about Anson intrigued her—that he occasionally worked at Bryce Canyon, of all the lovely places on earth. She was already making plans to go there soon, perhaps in the fall when the crowds were smaller and she could spend time in God's creation.

Bryce meant a great deal to her. It was the place where she encountered a personal God interested in her. Or rather He'd always had His eye on her, but she'd chosen to see Him for who He was. Not just in the fascinating hoodoo formations or in the other park features. But discovering that He loved her and cared about her. As the youth pastor said on the retreat long ago, God had shown the supreme act of love by sending His Son to die for her. It made a profound impact on Marissa's life, driving her to who she would become. Yes, Bryce Canyon was one of those places she thought of often and the place she wanted to revisit for a time of personal reflection.

But first things first. She took out the newspaper to circle some ads for a few job openings available in town. Most were temp jobs in gift shops, which Mom pressed her to check out. She needed to do something. Her savings wouldn't last forever, and she was beholden to her mother now that she had Sammy. Work, followed by an apartment, would help make her independent and settled.

"Oh Marissa, did I tell you that Wayne called?" Mom announced. "Something about dinner and a play tonight."

Dinner and a play? She didn't recall the invitation at first until she thought back to the coffee they had that one day and his interest in seeing a Shakespearean play during the annual summer festival. *Wayne! Uh oh.*

"Sounds like you two are getting along nicely," Mom added, venturing into the living room.

"Wayne's a nice guy, I guess. Though sometimes I feel like he's psychoanalyzing everything I say."

Mom laughed. "At least you're getting it done for free. Betty was telling me that he's settling here very well. He plans to have his office up and running in the fall when the college students return. Good thing, too."

"Why do you say that?"

"Kids have lots of stress at college. You did, didn't you?"

Marissa didn't want to confess to Mom that college meant freedom in many ways. There was the intensity of studies, yes, but there were good times, too, like being part of the ski team. She had a great time taking to the slopes where she'd nurtured a relationship with Eric after they met in class. She recalled the times at the ski lodge on a break from the slopes, warming her cold toes before the fake gas fireplace, talking with him about everything. She wondered then if Anson liked to ski. *Stop thinking about him like that*, she chastised herself. Maybe she should be asking Wayne if he liked to ski instead. Did she only have this strange fascination for Anson simply because he looked a little like Eric? Or maybe the idea he'd opened the door for her to get Sammy and bought the dog food stirred things to life. But then again, Wayne had bought her coffee and a muffin not once but twice.

The phone shrilled. "Get that, will you, Marissa?" Mom called.

She swept it up to hear Wayne's voice on the other end. "Did you get my message about the play? I tried your cell but just got voicemail."

"Is it really tonight?"

"I thought I told you what day it was back at The Grind, but maybe I didn't. Yes, the tickets are for tonight. Is that a problem?"

"I guess not." She looked at Sammy standing before the kennel door, staring longingly as if he couldn't wait for her to take him out of there and cuddle him. "Hey Wayne, do you like dogs?"

"Dogs? Sure, I like dogs. I don't own one myself, but I like them. We always had cats. Pets are very beneficial to their owners. Helps alleviate stress."

"You'll have to come by and see my new puppy. His name is Sammy."

"Sammy?"

"I named him after the seal. You know the children's book, *Sammy the Seal*? I mean, he doesn't look like a seal at all, but it was my favorite book when I was learning to read." She wondered if he would now psychoanalyze this.

"People find comfort in clinging to things from their childhood. It gives them a sense of security."

Is that bad? she wondered. She couldn't tell from his voice. Did he think she was searching for comfort? Or was she simply being a child at heart?

"Marissa, are you still there?"

"Yes, I'm here. So what time is this thing?"

"Our 'thing' starts at eight. I thought we could grab a bite to eat beforehand. I could pick you up at six."

Marissa was on his first sentence—the "thing" part. Did they have some "thing" going? Did agreeing to see the play set "things" in motion?

"Marissa? You don't seem like yourself today. Did you run into that man again or something?"

How would he know that? Was he spying on them? Or was it the psychologist in him at work once again? "Well yeah, but. . ."

"I could tell by your preoccupation. Listen, if you want my advice, which is pretty sound if I do say so myself, you need to stay away from him. It's creating negative feelings in you that are affecting both you and those around you. The further you keep away, the better it will be in coping with your loss."

"That may be a little hard considering Anson lives on a nearby street and walks his dog every day. Anyway, I thought it would be good running into him. Helps me deal with those bad feelings face-to-face instead of pretending they don't exist."

There was silence on the other end for a moment or two. "Actually it will keep reminding you of the feelings instead of moving past them. Anyway, what about your life now? For instance, you said you wanted to find an apartment. I can help you look tomorrow, if you want."

"I need a job first."

"I've been thinking about that. You could work for me. Do you know any secretarial skills? I need a receptionist."

Now wouldn't that be cozy. The mere image of them working side-by-side made her heart jump and her palms sweat. "Yes, I do know some secretarial skills, but Mom circled some ideas in the paper that I might take a look at first."

Again there was silence. Marissa sensed that things were not heading off on the right foot with Wayne, especially if they were supposed to be going out on a date later tonight. Finally he said okay and that he would see her at six. She sighed. So far this was already turning into a mixed-up day, and it was only nine o'clock in the morning. Not a great way to start.

Marissa opened the kennel and picked up Sammy. The pup nestled in her arms as if content to remain there. She cuddled him close and gave him a kiss on a furry cheek. "You're a good pup, ol' champ. And we'll find ourselves a place to call home. Once I get the job set. Which reminds me, I'd better start looking. Nothing will happen with me sitting around holding you." She gave the pup another kiss and returned him to his crate.

An hour later Marissa was pounding the pavement of the downtown area. She came to a small shop selling soaps and perfumes to find an older woman hanging up a HELP WANTED sign. Marissa immediately introduced herself.

"I know your mother. Rosie Jones. She said you were coming back to town and that you'd lost your husband."

"Well, he wasn't my husband, but we were engaged."

"I'm so sorry. Anyway, do you need a job? I can offer you temporary employment for the summer season. But if business is good, it may last until Christmas."

Marissa decided it was better than nothing. At least she was establishing a foothold in the realm of working society. And she would smell good after a day in a fragrant shop. She thanked the woman, Mrs. Holden, for the opportunity, filled out the necessary paperwork, and received a brief tour of the shop's inventory that included soaps, lotions, poofy sponges, baskets, and running the cash register.

Marissa then continued along the street until she came to the edge of the college campus. She found the large theater built on the college grounds that hosted the festival each summer, modeled after the Shakespearean Globe Theater with its English-style architecture. Expectation welled up within her at the planned evening with Wayne. She would take it all in stride and without any preconceived notions. Enjoy a quiet dinner and attend the performance. *Nothing to fret over and everything to look forward to*, she told herself. If only she could believe it.

❧

Marissa was determined to enjoy the evening, even if her mind was in a whirlwind with Mom, Sammy, Anson, and everything in between. It began well enough with dinner in a nice restaurant. Wayne talked about his family and how their mothers loved the craft club. He chatted about his college days, his first job trying to use his psychologist skills that nearly ended in disaster. For a guy, he did like to talk about himself, a quality Marissa didn't recall from their time in high school. Maybe because he spent all day listening to clients spout their troubles. He had no one to hear his life's stories. And for her part, she listened as best she could, smiling at the appropriate times while slowly eating a Caesar salad sprinkled with fresh croutons.

When dinner ended, Wayne announced they would need to head for the theater. When they arrived, the preshow was in full swing out front, with the actors and actresses singing, playing lutes and harps, and even a woman in Shakespearean garb selling fruit tarts from a tray. Marissa was instantly caught up in it all. She enjoyed being transported to another world for the time being, away from the things that had burdened her these many weeks and months.

But as the play got underway, she realized perhaps *Romeo and Juliet* wasn't the most endearing tale to encourage her heart at this time. She said nothing to Wayne about it during the intermission when they took a walk in the courtyard, stretching their legs and enjoying the pleasant evening. Instead she talked about the professional acting and the costumes. "After what I did in the theater in Omaha, I can only imagine how difficult it must be to put on a major production like this."

"Many of these actors and actresses go on to star on Broadway or other big-name shows," Wayne added. "They are multitalented. As for me, I could never act on a stage."

"It can get a little nerve-racking," she admitted. "But it's also fun. You develop friendships with those who are in the show. You become a family, wanting to see the show go on, to do a performance the audience will never forget."

The time outside rejuvenated her for the remainder of the play. Marissa settled in her seat, determined to enjoy the rest of the evening. At the play's conclusion, when Romeo and Juliet each took their lives by succumbing to poison and a knife, a strange feeling swept over her. It was difficult to take in—the idea of death in love. Even upsetting, as she squirmed inside.

She looked over at Wayne, who seemed mesmerized by it all. When the play concluded, he was all smiles. "What an excellent production. Though I knew it would be. It's never been less than stellar."

Marissa managed a small smile as they wandered through the throng before finding a quiet place on the darkened street.

"Anything wrong?"

"Oh, it was a great night, Wayne. Thank you so much for asking me to go."

"I must admit *Romeo and Juliet* can be an emotional experience. But it's interesting to see that when one makes up their mind for the challenge of love, they will do whatever is needed to see it happen. And I find it admirable as well that their hearts' desire was to reunite their stricken families. And though they did die, the goal was fulfilled in the end."

Marissa didn't know what to say. Maybe she was tired of death. She wanted life. Something to hold on to. She couldn't wait then to see her dog, Sammy. And Anson even. Maybe he would be walking Goldie tomorrow morning. Then she remembered that he was in Zion National Park.

Just then she felt warmth come calling. Wayne had picked up her hand as they walked along and now held it firmly in his. She allowed the contact for the time being. It had been a nice evening after all, and they'd had a good time together.

On the drive home they said little. Just shy of Mom's house, Wayne brought the car to a stop. He turned to face her. "I hope we can get together again soon. And I'd love to have you work for me, so please consider it. I can think of no one better I'd like by my side. We'd make a great team."

"Oh Wayne, I didn't tell you. I found a job today, at a gift shop. I appreciate all you've done for me, though." She turned aside, even as his gaze lingered. She felt the wisp of a light touch as his hand slowly turned her face to meet his.

"Marissa?" He stared, perusing her every feature. His head tipped to one side, his face leaning closer, his eyelids closing. His arms drew her toward him.

She struggled out of his embrace and grabbed the door handle. "I'd better go. Good night, Wayne." She left the car and headed swiftly for the house, imagining his startled reaction, perhaps even anger that he'd been denied a kiss. Of course after a romantic Shakespearean tale, even if it did end in tragedy, he would expect a kiss to cap off the night. He probably thought he deserved it. But she could not deliver. And it was just as well. She wasn't certain about walking any romantic path right now. She wanted to take it a step at a time, not at a swift jog.

Mom had already gone to bed. Marissa opened the door to hear a high-pitched whine. She saw Sammy standing on his little legs, wagging his stumpy tail furiously. She picked him up and carried him into the backyard to do his business. A million stars greeted her from a backdrop of pure ebony. She wondered if Anson was enjoying a starlit evening over Zion with its massive sandstone walls. Or even at Bryce Canyon with a full moon veiling the famous formations in pure white.

A chill fell over her. Maybe that's why she couldn't kiss Wayne tonight. She had too much of Anson on her mind. *Lord, help me settle my heart as I'm settling here in Cedar City. Most of all, help me find my way.*

seven

"Glad it worked out so you could be a part of our ministry here at the Jamboree, Anson."

Anson looked over at the smiling face of Pastor Ray, who went back to retrieve another case of water. The crowds slowly began to gather to celebrate the festivities. Along the streets were various booths—from homemade crafts and food to games and carnival rides. In front of the booths, lining the street, were automobiles of all makes and models from years' past. The event drew thousands of people to Cedar City's Main Street. And each year the church manned a booth where they gave out tracts and bottled water to thirsty Jamboree attendees.

"I am, too. Did I tell you my work schedule just changed? That means I can hang around weekends more. And show up for church more often."

"Good news. We've missed you. And I've been thinking of you, actually. There are a few events coming up that you might want to consider lending a hand with. Like the annual teen retreat late next month. I want to take the kids to Bryce. And since you know the park so well, I thought you might even want to head it up."

"Sounds good." He opened his mouth, ready to tackle the main subject on his heart—Marissa—when Pastor Ray walked off to retrieve another case of bottled water. Anson turned to peruse the sign-up sheet for manning the booth and stopped short when he saw a familiar name. *Marissa*

Jones. 2 p.m. "Marissa is working the booth?" he wondered, unaware that he'd spoken out loud until he heard Pastor Ray.

"Marissa came to town a few weeks ago. She visited our church last Sunday for the first time and wanted to help. It's good for her to become involved. You know her fiancé died tragically, which is why she came back here to Cedar City. Her mother lives here."

"I heard about that." Anson then noticed the blank space on the sign-up sheet beside Marissa's name. When Pastor Ray wasn't looking, Anson added his name in the time slot. He then hurried off to bring out more water. He wondered what she would think when she saw him in the booth. Well, what did it matter? They were doing it for the town and for God. Sharing the Gospel and handing out water. And it might give him an opportunity to learn more about her and her about him.

"So is work going well?" Ray inquired.

"As well as can be expected. The usual visitor issues."

"You look like something's on your mind."

He cast the man a glance, wondering how he deduced that.

"Look, Anson, I'll be honest. Carl and I have been meeting on occasion, and he did say you might be having some relationship issues. If I can be of any help. . .I know a little about this kind of thing." He offered a grin. "And I have a fairly good track record, too, when it comes to men finding their chosen spouses in the Lord. Not that I'm some spiritual matchmaker. But God has a way of using a multitude of counselors to help us come to important decisions. I can certainly pray for you. And I'm here if you want to talk about things."

Anson appreciated the offer and told him so. It was all new waters to him, not only in relationships but also the added burden of one who had been through a tragic loss. And the loss of a fiancé, no less. The memories were still fresh, as he noted on their initial encounter on the canyon walk. He wondered how another man could fit into the picture of Marissa's life. If her heart was open to receive. If his heart was ready to accept.

"Hello! Anyone manning this booth?"

He turned to see Lucy standing there with her two sons. He grinned. "Hey, Luce. Hey, Tommy and Chris." He opened the cooler and took out water for them. "I'd hand you a pamphlet, but I think you're already on the right side of godly things, huh?"

She smiled and took the bottled water. "How's work?"

Anson wondered if that was the proverbial question of the day to loosen things up. "They had me checking on a safety issue with one of the trails in Zion. Of course I had a group of tourists from Germany asking why the trail was closed when they'd flown across the ocean to hike it. I gave them my all-American smile."

"You're so full of yourself." Lucy shook her head with a grin as she twisted off the cap and drank some water. "So are you working the booth right now?"

"Actually I'm not scheduled until two. And we're basically set up here. So if you want me to take a pair of rambunctious nephews around, I'd be happy to."

"Thanks. I was hoping you'd say that. I'm sure they don't care to go cruising craft booths, looking at pot holders and handmade wreaths."

When she told the boys Anson would take them around the Jamboree, they each tugged on his hands. "Let's go look at the cars, Anson!" they chimed together.

He smiled and led them to the cars on display—from an

old-fashioned Packard to a modern-day Porsche and Bugatti. He bought them hot dogs and popcorn. They stopped at a booth where Jamboree-goers could throw darts at balloons for prizes.

"Can we, Anson?" asked Chris.

"Sure, why not?" He wouldn't mind hurling a dart himself to build up some confidence. He plunked down the money. One after the other they threw the darts until Chris successfully popped the very last balloon. He got a small picture of a rodeo rider for his trouble. Anson then paid for his own round of darts and took care of all the balloons in rapid succession, earning a huge wooly sheep for his skill.

"You're so cool, Anson. Wait till Mom sees what you won."

Anson had to admit he was surprised and a bit sheepish himself lugging the stuffed prize around. "Speaking of your mom, we'd better find out where she is, as I've got the church booth to man in about twenty minutes." He searched the crowds milling about until he found her, petite and brunette, examining a handmade trinket.

Lucy walked out of the booth and stopped short. She burst out laughing. "Anson, what in the world? Why do you have that huge stuffed sheep?"

"Anson busted five balloons in a row!" the boys chorused in unison.

"Wow. I didn't know you had it in you."

"And look what I won, Mom!" Chris announced, holding up his revered picture.

Lucy smiled at them and then, as if on cue, led Anson over to one side while the boys hovered at a nearby booth, examining marshmallow shooters made of plastic pipes. "So I guess it went well."

"Very well. They are also fine manipulators in ordering

food and prizes." He looked over at her to see her studying him intently. And again he sensed a similar distance as in their last face-to-face encounter. One he couldn't understand, as if she dearly wanted to break down a door existing between them but held back. What was it about the look on a woman's face that could send a multitude of different messages? He'd seen it in many places. With the rangers at Cedar Canyon. With Marissa on the canyon walk. Even his good friend, Diane, the cleaning lady at the Bryce Canyon Lodge. And now Lucy. Like they had some hidden agenda one must discover.

"So you aren't reading anymore obituaries, are you?" she asked, staring at the sheep he held under one arm.

"No. Nothing I want to make a habit of. I was just curious to learn more about Marissa's background."

"Not sure what you can learn from that."

He wanted to say how much Marissa obviously loved Eric and how that might be a cause for concern for anyone new trying to enter the scene. He hoped in time that would not be an issue.

She then asked, "Have you ever seen a picture of this woman's fiancé?"

Anson hesitated. "No, can't say that I have. There was no photo in the listing. Wouldn't it be interesting to see one, though, after she said we looked alike."

"Huh. I'll never forget my piano teacher saying I once looked like her long-lost cousin—a famous violinist at age thirteen." Lucy laughed until she broke out into hiccups. She then ordered Tommy to return the marshmallow shooter to the barrel where he got it, even as he showed it first to her and then to Anson.

"Please, can I have it? Please, Anson?"

Anson grinned. "If I gave in and bought that, Tommy, your

mother would not be happy." He took out his wallet. "Guess I'll have to get her a pot holder to ease the pain."

The boys yelped in glee as they took the money to buy the shooters. Lucy only shook her head.

"I'm trying to earn my title of uncle-of-the-year," he said with a wink.

"Well, they won't have much ammunition because I don't intend to get the marshmallows to use with them. And"—she paused and wagged her finger at him—"don't you dare think of getting them a bag of marshmallows either, little brother."

They both shared laughter until Anson realized it was time to head back to the church booth. "Stop by and meet Marissa when you can," he invited.

"Maybe I will."

Anson returned to the booth in time to relieve the two people manning it. He began piling the pamphlets into neat stacks. When he turned around, Marissa was in the back of the booth, stashing her purse behind some boxes. "What's this huge stuffed sheep doing here?" When she stood, they bumped into each other. "Oh, excuse me. . . ," she began. "Anson! What are you doing here?"

He thought he saw her visibly tremble, or maybe it was his imagination. He pointed to the sign-up sheet. "We're both manning the booth at two p.m."

"Oh." She pushed back strands of loose hair that had fallen out of the ponytail. "I didn't know anyone else had signed up. But I'm glad you did. I didn't want to do this alone."

"Jesus sent His disciples two by two. Or rather two plus three. The sheep in the back is mine. I won it tossing darts with my nephews."

She looked back at the sheep and couldn't help but grin. "I didn't know you went to this church. I thought you were like most everyone else in town, involved in the other religion, of which there seems to be a church on every corner."

He shook his head. Was that a sigh of relief he heard? "What about Wayne? What does he believe?"

"How do you know Wayne?"

Oops. "I. . .uh. . ." He realized she hadn't seen him watching them at the coffee shop a while back. "Oh, you start to know everyone in this town. Even the new people who come along. And I'll admit, I saw you drinking coffee a few weeks back— the day I showed you the ad for the puppies."

She nodded. "I've met so many new people. Especially at church. I want to be a part of the young adult group there. I was supposed to get in contact with these two girls I knew from high school, but it hasn't worked out. One of them is pregnant and pretty sick. So friends have been few until recently."

He hoped that meant she was considering him on the friendship angle. Which could be the start of something special, in time.

A couple came up then, and Marissa handed them bottles of water along with a smile. They shook their heads at the literature offered and said they were satisfied with their religion. "It isn't easy being a Christian here in town, I see," she remarked.

"Well, like most things, you stick to what you know and be salt and light wherever God places you."

A young college-aged student came up, and from the look in his eye, Anson figured he had something important to get out of his system. The guy began spouting out observations on the deity of Jesus and how their religions differed. Anson responded gently but firmly about the way Jesus had changed his life. How Jesus had been sent to bridge the gap between sinful men and God. When the young man walked off, clearly troubled, Marissa was staring at him.

"Wow. You're so good at this, Anson. Have you ever thought about becoming a pastor? Or going on missions?"

"Actually, Pastor Ray wants me to help lead the teen group when they go to Bryce Canyon later this summer."

"What? The church youth group is going to Bryce Canyon? When? I want to help. In fact, I must!"

Anson saw a fire ignite her dark and lovely eyes. More hair had fallen out of her ponytail. She undid the band, her hair cascading about her shoulders, before she caught it up once more behind her head. He stood there staring at it all. If only they hadn't gotten off on the wrong foot that first day on the canyon walk. If only the day could be repeated for the better, and they could start fresh. Like today.

She wiped her hand across her face, turned aside, and shook her head. "Oh wow. God, help me please."

Anson stepped back, startled. "I. . .I'm sorry. I didn't mean to stare. You have nice hair is all."

"It's not your fault. It's just at that moment you looked so much like. . ." She paused. "You reminded me of Eric, the way he used to look at me." She began thumbing through the stack of brochures. "But that isn't fair. I really need to get a handle on this once and for all."

"It's okay." He forced away any frustration at the continued comparisons. Eventually the man would fade from her thoughts, if he was patient. He smiled instead as more people stopped by for water on this hot afternoon. Pastor Ray dropped by also to make sure they had enough of everything. Anson and Marissa said little else for the next fifteen minutes. He wished the time hadn't deteriorated into another "Eric" moment for her. It had been going so well. He thought great strides were being made. But the past remained an ever-present shadow that left a dark imprint.

"So how's it going, Marissa?"

Anson looked up to see a tall guy with dark hair lean over the table in a causal stance. *Great.* To add another fateful twist to the day, Wayne Newberry had decided to make a sudden appearance. The broad grin on his face betrayed his distinct interest in Marissa. "I was hoping you'd be able to go around the Jamboree with me." He said nothing to Anson.

"I still have another forty minutes to work, Wayne. It's a two hour shift."

"I can handle it if you want to go," Anson offered, but then wondered why he'd said it. Did he really want this guy latching onto her? Why didn't he push her to stay and work the entire shift?

"You've been reprieved." Wayne nodded his thanks to Anson.

"I'll go in about twenty minutes, okay? I want to at least start to finish what I began."

He opened his mouth as if to counter her, then clamped his lips shut and walked off.

"It's okay if you want to go," Anson said.

"Yes, but I signed up to do this. It's not right that he can peel me away from a commitment that I've made. Though it's nice of you to volunteer."

"Sure, no problem." He wished then Wayne wasn't in the equation of her life. He'd really like to ask her out for a bite to eat. Or another walk in the canyon. He'd even drive her to her beloved Bryce Canyon and take her to every overlook. He had some Bryce mementos at home, given to him by the concessionaire at the end of the season last year. Maybe he could give her something, like a key chain or some coasters. "So why do you like Bryce Canyon so much?"

"I accepted Christ into my heart at the canyon rim."

"Really."

"I was on a youth retreat, kind of what the pastor is planning for the teens at church. It was amazing. I'd just heard this great testimony from another youth minister on how he'd accepted Christ on an outdoor trip. We were looking at the scenery at sunset. You know that Bryce looks best at sunrise and sunset."

"Yes." *And you would, too. I can see it in my mind, with the fading sunlight reflecting in your hair. Wow.* He silenced his drifting thoughts.

"I was at one of the overlooks, and He became real in His creation. He wasn't a book or a church. God wanted me to know Him personally. It's hard to put into words."

"Yes," he said again, thinking how much he would like to run his fingers through her luxurious hair. *Knock it off.*

"Now with everything that's happened, I'd like to go back there and see what God has new for my life. And to answer any leftover questions."

"Like why your fiancé died?"

She turned. Her eyes widened slightly, revealing the appealing mocha color of them. "That could be. Maybe. I do wonder why he was called to heaven so early in life. And after we had made so many plans."

"God may tell you why. And He may not. Are you ready for either answer?"

She didn't reply. After another five minutes, Wayne reappeared, holding a melting ice cream cone, which he gave to her, accompanied by a charming smile. Anson had to hand it to Wayne for cleverly buying ice cream in an effort to lure her out of the booth. And it worked. Marissa gave Anson one final look before drifting off into the crowds. He watched her disappear while thinking on her words.

Suddenly Lucy and the nephews were standing before the booth. "Who was that, Anson?" Lucy asked. "Marissa?"

"Yes."

"She's a lovely girl."

He thought so, too. But now her lovely form clung to another man's arm.

"If God wants it to happen, it will. If not, you have to trust Him."

He looked over at her. "What was that?"

"You and Marissa. I saw her going off with that other guy. You remember the guy I was dating when Frank came on the scene. But there was nothing like Frank. Just as I believe, if this is God, there will be no stopping things between you two. No matter who or what comes on the scene."

Lucy, you've read my heart. But only God can make it happen, like you say. "Just for that, you get to take my sheep home."

She grinned. "Wow. Thanks a bunch."

eight

"So are you a Christian, Wayne?" Marissa couldn't believe how quickly the question came leaping out. But since the meeting with Anson, she had to know where things stood. They'd had a pleasant enough time at the Jamboree, even though she spent most of her time thinking about Anson. Now they were back at The Grind once more, perusing life. She'd already been through so much these many months; she didn't want to start out on a wrong foot and in a relationship that was not of the Lord. Here in Cedar City, like in most Utah towns, beliefs in God took on different meanings and led one on different roads. She wanted a man who believed like she did, in the deity of Christ and eternal life through His ultimate sacrifice for sinful man.

"What led you to ask me this? Talk about sudden."

She squirmed, wondering if he considered it a personal affront. Or if he would psychoanalyze her intentions. But to her, it was important. "I don't know. My relationship with Christ means a great deal to me. You probably know that by now, especially with the work at the church booth during the Jamboree."

"Yes, I can see that, which is fine. Religion is very comforting to many people. And I go to church, if that's what you wanted to know." He mentioned the one he sometimes attended. She asked a few more questions about his true beliefs, only to watch his fingers tighten around the mug of coffee and his face grow rigid.

Marissa began to play with the strap to her purse as the meaning behind it all began to peal loud and clear.

"So what's the real reason for this?" he asked. "I'm curious."

"Well, I was talking to Anson..."

"The guy in the booth." He paused. "You know him?"

"I've seen him a few times. He's a park ranger or something like that. He..." She hesitated, wondering if she should divulge any more about her encounters with Anson. She noticed Wayne's eyes narrow and his face redden. He was sensing competition. And Marissa was sensing confusion on her part. "We walk our dogs together. I met him a few times on the canyon walk. He has a dog, Goldie."

"This isn't the same guy you thought looked like your fiancé?"

She sat back, realizing Wayne was indeed good at putting pieces of situations together. In fact, it downright irked her. "I...well..."

"Look, Marissa, you can't do this to yourself. It's not healthy, linking up with a guy you think is your fiancé come back to life. I'm sure it makes him uncomfortable, too."

"Maybe at first, but he doesn't seem to mind. He actually understands."

Wayne frowned as if unhappy to hear this latest development. "Marissa, I know it takes time to grieve. You need to give yourself that time. The grieving process becomes unhealthy when you start imagining situations and people, like you did with this perfect stranger. If you want, I know the name of a good psychiatrist who can—"

Marissa jumped to her feet. "I don't need a psychiatrist!" She threw the strap of her purse over her shoulder. "I'm trying to work things out, thanks very much. But one thing's for sure—I don't need someone psychoanalyzing everything I say or do. I want the freedom to explain things without thinking I'm a perpetual patient."

His features softened. "You're right. I'm sorry if I've come across like that. I just don't want you hurting any more than you already are. I care about you, Marissa. More than you know."

She slowly sat back down but could not look him in the eye. His steady, piercing gaze could drag a person in and hold them.

"I have hopes that things might be starting up again for us. We had a satisfying and healthy relationship going at one time, if you remember."

Satisfying? Healthy? She tried to consider the few times they went out for pizza in high school. She recalled the one kiss they shared. Or maybe twice, if she counted the night of the prom.

"You were an awesome prom date, too. We got an award, if you remember, for the best-looking couple. I know you've been through a lot since then, but there's no reason to think the sparks aren't still there. I believe they are. And I think it's interesting that we both decided to move back to Cedar City at the same time."

But for Marissa, sparks left over from high school weren't enough to start anything, let alone the blaze of a relationship. She feigned the need to leave, thanked him for coffee, and headed out into the hot sun. Despite what Wayne thought, she'd really been thinking about Anson, and more than just occasionally. Daily might be a better way to frame it. She could not get out of her mind the passion in Anson's voice at the Jamboree when he shared the gospel message with visitors at the booth. He was definitely an intriguing man. But the way he stared at her that one moment in the booth when she was fixing her hair. . .that threw her for a loop. And made her wonder if Wayne could be right about one thing— that she was setting herself up for more heartache if she didn't first release the past. Not that she would forget Eric, but she would remember that his love was in another time and place. That it was time for new wine in new wineskins, as the Bible said.

Marissa arrived at the soap shop to be met with flowery scents that nearly sent her into a sneezing fit. Mrs. Holden welcomed her with a smile. Though she tried to concentrate on her work, Marissa could only think about the conversation with Wayne. Clearly he was vexed by her decision to suggest Christianity in their relationship. Not that Eric was the most outspoken in his beliefs. They attended a nice evangelical church in Omaha. They didn't talk that much about God. Sometimes they prayed together. But she knew he was a Christian and that God had brought them together. And just as quickly had torn them apart.

She rang up a few purchases that day, even as Mrs. Holden complained about the slow business. "I'm afraid if things don't start picking up, Marissa, I'm going to have to let you go. I already warned your mother about it. But I hear you can get a fine job working for Betty's son. Like a secretary or something. Maybe you should consider it."

Marissa sighed, wondering if along with making their crafts, the women in the craft club jabbered about their lonely children in need of relationships. "I. . .well, I don't know. I hope I can continue working here. I like this job very much."

"Well, don't you worry. Betty Newberry's son is quite well off. He's a doctor. But you already know that. Betty says you two have been on a few dates already." The older woman patted her arm.

"He's been very nice," she said politely before blowing out a sigh, wishing well-meaning people would stop pushing Wayne Newberry her way. Yes, he was a nice guy. Yes, he seemed interested in her welfare. Yes, he was buying a house and that meant money. But there were also negatives as well. Things she could not ignore.

When the day ended, Marissa walked slowly toward Mom's house, distracted by her thoughts. Until she realized Sammy would need to go for a walk soon, and she hurried to relieve him of the confining crate. "Let's go on the canyon walk today, Sammy," she informed the dog. It was nice to be so close to the picturesque walk that meandered along a river and into a rocky canyon carved by wind and water. She arrived to find others walking dogs, jogging, or just enjoying the summer evening. All at once she saw a familiar golden retriever mosey on past her. "I'd know that dog anywhere," she murmured.

She heard a laugh and turned to see Anson walking toward her. "Hi. This is the last day you'll see us. I'm off again to the parks in the morning." He spoke as if it was the most natural occurrence running into her again. And maybe it was, in God's great timing.

"I thought you might be gone already, being a Monday afternoon."

"I'm on a different schedule. Except I won't be in church next Sunday. They have me working a split weekend. I thought I was over that, too. They said this is the last one, and I'll be glad. I miss church."

Marissa enjoyed hearing Anson talk about his work in the parks and also his interest in church. He then paused to look at the river. Marissa stopped and stood beside him. She enjoyed his presence, his strength, the way he and the creation surrounding him seemed to fit so well together. The two dogs decided to lie down at that moment. Sammy nestled close to Goldie's tummy. The sight brought comfort and maybe a precursor of the future.

"Look at that," Anson noted with a chuckle. "Dogs know. They're already friends." His voice drifted off. Marissa wondered if Anson could use a friend. She certainly could. She had Wayne bugging her but no other real friends to speak of since coming here. She'd been too wrapped up in her new puppy and the poofy job at the soap store, among other things. "It's good to have friends to talk to."

"I'm glad for Carl. He's a great guy. I hope you're making a few friends at church. There's a women's group that meets weekly."

"Yeah. Haven't been there yet, though the pastor's wife, Alicia, invited me." Sammy then lay on his side, all fours spread out, looking to catch a few winks. Goldie did the same.

"You should go. One thing I've found out, it's important to have people to talk to. Especially coming from the situation you did." He paused. "I. . .well, the past is good to get out."

"I'd rather leave it alone and move on. Everyone seems to think I need to talk about it. But Eric's gone. It's over and done with. Even though I have to admit, every time I see you. . ."

"You still see your fiancé sometimes?" he wondered.

Her cheeks grew hot. "Sorry. It has to stop eventually. Either that or Sammy and Goldie will have to find new buddies."

"Marissa, it's okay. I really do understand. It takes time. I'd hate to let that come between our walks."

She stared down at her feet, wishing then she'd not spooked him that first day. "It was such a dumb thing to do to you, asking if you were Eric of all things. I wish I could have a do-over where that's concerned."

"Okay. Then let's." He faced her and extended his hand. "Hi, I'm Anson McGruder. Welcome to Cedar City."

She looked first at his large hand, tanned by the sun and wind, and then at his face. She shook it, chuckling softly.

He continued. "You may not realize this, but I'd like to get to know you a little better since we're neighbors and dog lovers and, yes, Christians who need to stick together when the going gets rough."

He then turned and looked back at the river. He was being a gentleman through and through. And what did he say—something about wanting to get to know her? The mere thought made her feel even warmer under the collar of her shirt, adding to the temperature of the late summer afternoon.

"Would you like to go out for dinner sometime?"

The invitation caught her completely off guard. She whirled.

"Thought I'd land that one on you. I know you're probably going out with other guys and everything. Just thought I'd ask. Give you something to think about while I'm at work this week." He took out his wallet and withdrew a business card. "Here's my phone number and e-mail address. If you prefer texting or e-mailing, I'll understand. Let me know if it will work out for you sometime."

"Okay." She looked at the picture of him smartly dressed

in a park uniform, appearing quite official. While he did resemble Eric in some ways, in the picture he was handsome and with his own extraordinary life. Anson McGruder, as he had said. She then heard him heave a sigh.

"I wish. . ." His voice drifted off.

Marissa wondered what he was about to say.

He turned to look at her, his mouth parted slightly, his hand extended. "Marissa, if you could only know how much. . ."

"Hey there!"

They turned to find a man striding up to them. Both dogs jumped up and barked greetings.

"Carl, what are you doing here?" Anson asked in astonishment. "I don't know you to walk much of anywhere, let alone here."

The man called Carl paused and looked between them both. "Ha. I figured I'd find you walking Goldie. But not taking a stroll with a fine lady." He held out his hand to Marissa. "Carl Bruce."

"Marissa Jones. Anson's mentioned you. He said you were good friends."

"I'm more like his conscience. Anyway, I'm here to tell you, Anson, that I can't keep Goldie this week. I was called out of town unexpectedly. Seems my company is doing a special trade show up in Salt Lake, and I have to leave early. I was going to call your cell but figured the walk would do me good."

Marissa saw Anson's face fall. "You can't keep Goldie this week. . . ," he repeated.

"Yeah, sorry about that."

Anson looked down at the dog sitting at his feet. "I can't put her in a kennel."

Marissa stared at both dogs sitting companionably with each other. Could she really do it? Would Mom have a coronary if she offered? "I might be able to keep her," she suddenly remarked.

Both men turned to face her. "You're going to save my reputation and my friendship if you could," Carl said with a grin.

Anson stared wide-eyed. "Wow, Marissa. This means a lot. I mean Goldie's no trouble. I can fill you in on everything. She's real easy to care for."

Carl waved at them, claiming he needed to get ready for his unexpected business trip. Anson continued to stare with more than relief on his face, but rather a look teeming with affection. He began describing Goldie's daily routine. "Do you think you can walk both dogs?"

"If not, I'll do one, then the other." She exhaled a sigh. "I just have to convince Mom it's a good idea."

"I'll pay you, of course. Eighty dollars for the week."

"You don't need to pay me."

"Actually, make it an even hundred."

"Anson, you don't need to. I'm more than happy to do it."

He stepped forward, looking as if he might supplement his gratefulness with something else. Dare she think he might kiss her by the way he'd settled his gaze on her lips? She stepped back, and he likewise retreated. "Okay, how about this? Will you go out to dinner with me when I get back as payment for watching Goldie?"

"All right." She smiled before taking the leash out of his hand. "C'mon, Goldie. Sammy. Let's see if this is going to work."

The two dogs leaped to their feet. Sammy, with his youthful exuberance, wanted to dash ahead, but Goldie kept him at an even walk.

Anson's laughter chased them down the path. "You're going to do just fine!" he called out.

The two dogs nuzzled each other's faces before stopping when she did, looking up as if to inquire if this arrangement might be permanent. "I think they will be all right."

Anson walked up and took Goldie's leash from her hand. Their fingers brushed. She lifted her gaze to see the deep blue of his eyes, matching the color of the sky above.

"I'll drop her off at seven," he said. "I hope that's not too early."

"I hope she'll be okay while I'm at work."

"No problem. She's as good as gold, hence the name Goldie."

Marissa chuckled. His fingers curled around hers and gave a small squeeze, sending tingles through her.

"Thank you so much. You're a godsend. Maybe in more ways than one."

They continued down the walk toward their respective homes. When Marissa came to her street, she offered a farewell.

"I'd be glad to come over to the house and introduce Goldie to your mom," Anson suggested.

"That's all right. It's only for a few days."

They stood looking at each other. A certain tension filled the air—of two hearts steadily developing an attraction for each other. Finally he said good-bye and turned toward his street. She watched him trot off at a fast pace with Goldie right beside him. She looked down at Sammy, who wagged his short, thin tail. "Well, we've got some fast talking to do.

Pray that God gives me the words to help calm Mom when she hears that another dog is going to be in the house." But that thought didn't concern her now. What filled her mind was Anson—the intimacy of the moment with his hand holding hers. Soon she would be ready to grab hold of the future and never let go.

nine

Every time I see you..., she began.

You still see your fiancé sometimes, he finished.

Anson thought about the conversation as he went about his business, this time at the popular Bryce Canyon National Park, where visitors littered the walkways and hovered at the overlooks, taking in the scenery of the mysterious canyon. He was considering Marissa more each day and wanted to take their budding friendship to the next level. The morning he dropped off Goldie, Marissa met him with a smile, claiming she'd convinced her mother to accept another dog if she helped paint the living room once everything was said and done. "A little finagling never hurt," she added, tossing back her thick, luxurious hair. He hoped he hadn't come on too strongly yesterday, insisting on dinner when he returned. Marissa didn't seem taken aback by it. She'd agreed to everything, after all. Even at the moment when he'd surrendered Goldie's leash to her perfectly manicured fingers complete with plum nail polish. Her steady smile followed him out the door. He only wished his interest in Marissa wasn't marred by obstacles still left to overcome. Another guy and the memory of a deceased fiancé among them.

"You haven't moved a muscle," a voice called out to him. Anson looked up to see his good friend Diane, who cleaned in the lodge. "You've been staring at the same scrap of paper for thirty minutes."

Anson finally noticed the papers strewn across the desk

he'd appropriated in a room at the main lodge. He hadn't even looked at the forms outlining new park safety regulations in the past half hour. The words were a blur to his befuddled mind. He cracked a smile. "Checking up on me again, huh, Diane?"

"Someone has to." Diane sat down opposite him, a knowing smile on her face. He knew her well from his time working in Bryce. She'd come here some twenty years ago to clean at the lodge and had been in the same position ever since. When he was new to the park scene, she'd befriended him, bringing him a tin of oatmeal cookies as a welcome gift. On occasion Anson bought her a cup of coffee when the dining room wasn't filled with customers, and they'd chat about life. She told him about her family and her three sons. He'd tell her mundane things about his boring life, along with updates on Goldie. But now his life had an unexpected twist in it and none of it boring.

"I happen to know you pretty well, Anson. What's up? I can see it in your face."

"I'm not sure where to begin."

"Whenever my sons had that look, there was usually a girl involved."

Anson looked away. "I, well. . ." Again a woman's perception amazed him, as if she could read his life in his eyes. He recalled a similar scenario at Cedar Breaks with the two inquisitive rangers. What was it about the female persuasion that sensed the unspoken?

"I raised three sons, you know. I've seen them go through every kind of situation with a girl there is. From moving in with one, to breakups, to marrying one of them. I know all the signs. So you asked her out, and she said no or something? She doesn't like you?"

"Actually I think she may like me. I'm not sure. There's another guy on the scene, too, and. . ."

Diane looked at him expectantly, waiting for the rest.

"I know we're not supposed to compare, but. . ."

The chair scraped. "Yes, that's right. You're a wonderful man, Anson, with many fine qualities."

"Yeah. Sometimes I wish I were her fiancé's double. Then I know she would take to me in an instant."

Diane stared. "What do you mean by that?"

"On the first day we met, she was fairly insistent that I was her fiancé come back to life. She'd lost him in an accident seven months ago, just before they were set to marry."

"Dear me. Maybe it's a blessing then that it's not working out, Anson. She sounds like someone you should be avoiding right now until things are better. She's obviously not over her fiancé. Maybe she needs some counseling."

"I don't think it's anything serious like that. And it's not what's causing me to pull back."

"It's the other man," she said with a nod. "Well, you'll have to do your best to win her heart, Anson. Like you won mine with a cup of coffee, making friends with a lady that could be your mother." She winked. "You have a good heart."

"I need someone to keep me on the straight and narrow."

"You already are. You just have to see yourself the way God does. That He has big plans for us. I'm not sure if yours includes this woman or not. But at least you're asking. And seeking. As the Bible says, seek and you will find when the door is open to you. It may not be that time right now. You hear what I'm saying?"

"Yes, I hear." It was heeding to faith and patience that was tough to follow.

Diane stood to her feet. "I just know you're going to find

your way and that special lady to share your life with, Anson. Even if some other man might be standing in the way. God has a way of moving mountains. If God could make this beautiful place of Bryce Canyon out of rock so others can cherish it, God can certainly make something beautiful out of your hard places. If you're patient, that is."

The words rang true, even if Anson fought to accept the entire meaning of it. He gathered the papers into a folder and tucked them into a soft-sided case beside his laptop. Wandering out into the open area of the lodge, he saw several couples walking around with smiles on their faces, holding hands or with arms around each other. He'd never considered other couples until this moment. Now he wanted a hand to hold. A face to grasp close. Lips to kiss. Someone to share the splendor of the evening sunset casting a reddish glow over Bryce Canyon.

He sighed. It made no sense to think about that now. He had two more days of work to get through. And then a wondrous dinner date when he returned to Cedar City. He waited in expectation and a hope that the door to Marissa's heart would soon open wide.

❧

Anson arrived on the doorstep of the Jones residence at six p.m. to hear barking inside. He then heard a woman's voice telling one of the pups to settle down, and she'd give the dog a treat. It didn't sound like Marissa's voice, but then again he wasn't sure what her voice sounded like behind closed doors. When he knocked, he heard footsteps, and the door swung wide before him. An older woman stood there with her hair a tangled mess, a grim look on her face. "Yes?"

"I'm Anson McGruder. We've met before, at the grocery store."

"Oh, yes. I think I've seen you around town." She looked in a hurry.

"I'm here to pick up Goldie." He paused. "My dog?"

"Oh, thank goodness. It's about time. Those animals are driving me crazy. I don't know that much about dogs. I mean, I did take care of Marissa's sick dog when she ran off to be with that other man. But these two, they were something else. Marissa had to work overtime tonight, or she would be here."

Anson stepped inside to survey the humble, one level ranch home. Goldie bounded up to him and put her front paws on his legs in a greeting. "Hey it's okay, I'm back." He then moseyed on out to the kitchen to see the woman taking food out of the fridge. "Do you have her leash and food bowls, Mrs. Jones?"

"I don't know where any of those things are. Marissa was supposed to take care of it all. Just look around. I'm sure you'll find them somewhere."

Anson stepped back into the living room, scanning the place, when his gaze fell on a picture of a couple atop a bookcase. He peered closer. The woman was Marissa. And then he saw himself standing beside her, her head resting against his shoulder. He jumped back, and when he did, he fell over Goldie and onto the floor.

"For heaven's sake!" Mrs. Jones cried, running out. "What happened? Did you hurt yourself?"

"I. . ." He rose gingerly to his feet, feeling a twinge in his tailbone. "Sorry. I—I was looking at the picture there on the bookcase and didn't see Goldie behind me."

"It's Marissa's engagement photo that she put in the paper. That's her with Eric, the one she was going to marry. I feel badly about what happened to him, but I'm glad she was able to move back here. She was too far away, living in Omaha."

He hesitated, then said, "I've never been to Omaha."

"Neither have I. But that's where Eric's family lives, so I guess he wanted to be there. Though usually the bride picks her own family to live nearby. I always thought so, anyway." She paused, staring first at him, then at Eric. "My goodness."

He sensed it. Tension. A certain strangeness. Perhaps even a sense of foreboding. "Mrs. Jones?"

"Why, you look just like him!"

Anson's face heated up quicker than an iron. He wanted to grab Goldie's leash and run, but his feet remained frozen. "Guess it's just one of these things," he managed to say.

"I guess so. Wow, it's uncanny. I can't get over it. How about that?"

He began looking around once more for Goldie's leash, wishing Rosie Jones wouldn't stare at him that way.

Suddenly the door opened, and Marissa burst in. She stopped short. "Anson! I forgot you were picking up Goldie today."

"Yes, and those two dogs nearly drove me to the insane asylum," Mrs. Jones grumbled. "But it's even more crazy. Just look at this, Marissa!" To Anson's horror, she thrust the engagement photo before Marissa's nose. "Look at this! Now look at him. Can you believe it? The eyes. And the nose and jaw. I'm telling you, they could pass as twins. If you change the hairstyle and dress them the same. I knew twins when I went to school. Dressed alike, you couldn't tell them apart."

The air left him. He had to make his escape and soon before this escalated into something he'd rather not face. He thanked them quickly for Goldie's care and hustled out, only to hear Marissa call for him.

"Anson."

He turned and looked at her.

"I'm sorry about what Mom said. I don't know why she did that. Maybe she's afraid I'll take off again or something, if you look like Eric."

For once he was speechless. And unnerved. "You don't think I'm your fiancé come back to life, do you?"

She stood staring, her mouth dropping open. "Of course not. I was dumb to do that to you when we first met. I really hope we can forget about it."

But was it truly dumb? Especially after what just happened with her mother? Maybe they all wished this Eric were alive. That he was resurrected in Anson. And that to Anson was as creepy as any tale from the deep. Of course he did believe in the resurrection on the last day, as the Bible describes. But he wasn't that guy. Or anyone else. He was Anson McGruder. At least he prayed he still was.

"I don't know what else to say, but I'm willing to let it go," she said softly. "Okay, so you look like him in certain ways. But that's not why I like you. I like you for who you are. Nothing more, nothing less."

That alone should have sent his spirits soaring. If only he did not glance back at the window to see a shadow standing there, staring. Her mother. Maybe still holding the picture and shaking her head. *God, what am I going to do?* He knew what he had to do. Leave Marissa to Wayne and anyone else who could help. And not look back. His feet obeyed, but his heart did not. He turned once more to look back at the house. Marissa had disappeared. But her presence was even more alive and real to him. And so, too, were her expressive eyes. And her voice that told him none of this mattered, that her heart was ready to accept him. Then why did he have this stigma attached to him? How would it help propel a relationship anywhere except to no-man's-land?

God, what am I supposed to do? He sat down on the curb. Goldie promptly sat down beside him. He took out his cell. Call Pastor Ray? Or Carl? Carl would hoot and holler and tell him he should have left well enough alone. Maybe Lucy could impart a woman's perspective on this. He pressed her number but was met with a busy signal. Probably better. No sense heaping his troubles on everyone else. He tugged on the leash, bringing Goldie to her feet. He had no choice but to wait for now.

ten

Marissa hustled to the soap store. She was glad for the job to take her mind off the encounter with Anson, which rattled her more than she cared to admit. A good many tourists were out and about this hot day, which bode well for business in the store. Mrs. Holden was sure to be happy, as tourists meant money coming into the small boutique. And money meant Marissa could hold on to this job until something better opened up. Or maybe she should continue with her education and become a teacher—a career she once dreamed about when she was little.

She hurried inside and stowed away her purse, then saw the owner arranging a new set of lavender "Sleep So Nice" bath products on a shelf.

"What's the matter, dear?" asked Mrs. Holden. "You look preoccupied."

"I'm fine, thanks." She could never speak about what was happening, especially to Mrs. Holden, a fellow member of Mom's craft club. Not that Mrs. Holden wouldn't know eventually, as word spread like a wildfire in the craft club. She could see it now—Mom bringing the engagement photo to the next club meeting as if it were show-and-tell, exclaiming how Anson was a mirror image of Eric. And that meant Marissa should have nothing to do with him or any man that happened to pop into her life. Unless it was appropriate for the marriage radar screen, like Wayne Newberry. And Mrs. Newberry would be there, nodding her head in agreement and telling Mom to do whatever she could to put a snag in the relationship and get things going with Wayne. Marissa bit her lip, wishing she wouldn't entertain these thoughts. But it irritated her the way others wanted to run her life. As if she couldn't allow God to help her navigate her way through the road of a relationship, even if that road proved rather rocky.

The morning was busy, allowing her to keep her thoughts on explaining bath products to customers rather than on other things. Then the door to the shop opened, and, to her surprise, Anson walked in. Marissa smoothed the loose strands of hair behind her ears, wishing she had time to spruce up her lipstick. She pushed aside any thought of their last encounter and willed herself to greet him. "Well, stranger. What brings you to a place like this?"

Anson looked around in interest and inhaled deeply. "Ahh. I'm trying to find out what it is I'm smelling. I can't decide if it's strawberry or roses. . ."

"Probably a mixture, I'm sure. We have strawberries and roses, among the dozens of other scents. And Mrs. Holden just got done putting a display together of lavender products. Supposedly that's good for relaxation."

"Really. I wouldn't mind seeing some. I'm getting a gift for Lucy."

Who was Lucy? She racked her brain as she led him over to the display, trying to remember if he'd mentioned a Lucy. Was she like Wayne was to her—an acquaintance from the past?

"Did you hear what I said?" He stared at her in puzzlement.

"What? Sorry, I've got a lot of things on my mind today."

"I was wondering if you thought a basket of these lavender products might make a good birthday gift."

"Oh, of course. She can spray some of the fragrance on her pillow at night to help her relax. And of course, the shower gel and lotion are relaxing as an evening bath."

"Wonder what Frank will think of the pillow thing," he said aloud, then backpedaled with a sheepish apology.

Marissa was still trying to understand who these people were.

"Frank's her husband," he added as if to answer her unspoken question. "And if he's anything like me, he doesn't know much about fragrances. I mean I take showers and brush my teeth, but I've never been one to slap on the fancy cologne. Or perfume my pillow." He chuckled, then turned serious. "I can see you're distant today."

"Sorry, I don't mean to be." For Marissa, she was on the idea that the woman was a relation, and she needn't have to allow the ugly green monster to emerge. Was she really jealous of another woman in Anson's life? What did that say about where Anson stood in her heart? *A lot*, she answered herself.

"And I'm sorry we ended up missing out on that dinner I promised you. Things kind of got out of hand the other evening. Any chance you're free for lunch? It will soon be that time. If I buy this nice big basket for my sister, do you think your boss will let you have an hour with me?"

Marissa stole a glance at Mrs. Holden, who was observing them with interest from the cash register. "I'm sure this purchase will make a big impression, on both Mrs. Holden and Lucy."

He smiled, picked up the basket, and headed over to the register. In a few minutes, he returned and offered her his elbow. "You're all set. She needs you back here by one."

"I never heard of making an exorbitant purchase just to

take someone out to lunch. This is going to cost you more than you know."

"Lucy deserves it. She's a terrific sis. Maybe the basket will say it all when the words don't."

"I think it's a very loving gesture that she will surely appreciate. And I'm sure she's loved having you as a brother, even with the sibling differences. My sister Phyllis and I get along pretty well, even though she's five years older than me."

"Hmm. Same with us. Lucy is five years older than me. We did have our moments. And sibling squabbles. But I guess so does everyone. Except she did like to boss me around sometimes."

"Yes! I know exactly what you mean." Marissa stepped closer.

"And made me play school where she was the teacher and could give me an *F* for poor penmanship."

"Oh, Phyllis was merciless. And then I found out I'd rather be the teacher. In fact, I'd love to go back to school and become one."

"You should." He looked around the soap shop. "This place smells nice, but it isn't one of those long-term professions one can count on in life. Did you teach in Omaha?"

She shook her head. "No, I worked in a store there, too. I don't have my master's yet, and they prefer that for teaching. I guess I was too interested in the marriage degree. Too much too soon." She lapsed into silence.

After putting the basket in his car, he looked up and down the street. "Is a sandwich shop okay?"

"That would be fine."

She followed him to a shop and the counter where they ordered wraps and iced green tea. When their orders came, Anson led the way to a corner table. He said a prayer, then began eating. They made small talk while he finished his sandwich in record time. "Guess I was hungry. I didn't eat breakfast."

"So what do you do on your days off?"

"Plenty to do around my house, fixing up things. I have an older place, so there's always something that needs repair. I hang out with Carl, and sometimes we play racquetball at the college gym. Maybe I can begin hanging out with you more often." He winked. She couldn't tell if he was kidding or being serious. "Actually, I'm going to have more things to do in the coming week. Like getting ready for this big trip."

"Are you going somewhere?"

"The church teen group is going on a retreat, and Pastor Ray asked me to help. Since I know Bryce Canyon so well, he wants me to help lead it. I've been making plans for meals, devotions, things we will do while we're there. . . ."

"Bryce Canyon! That's right, I remember you saying something about that at the Jamboree." She could barely contain her excitement, even as her reaction sparked wide eyes and a grin on Anson's face. "I think I did tell you how much that park means to me."

"I do recall a hint to that effect." His smile broadened. And then his eyes turned misty, displaying a certain tenderness as if he liked what he saw.

"So do you need any help? I didn't do too much with the youth in the church I attended in Nebraska, but I do love Bryce and would like to help."

"Do you know anything about camping? Making pancakes over a propane stove? Things like that?"

"Uh. . ." How could Marissa tell him she wasn't a camper by any stretch of the imagination. Camping to her was slow room service at the Marriott. "You're camping?"

"Yes. We'll bring tents and sleeping bags. We'll cook over a propane stove."

"Wow, you really are roughing it." She hesitated. "I think we did the same thing when I was part of the youth outreach long ago. It was like one overnight. Mostly I remember the message that led me to Christ."

Anson's features softened. His head tipped to one side. "Then you should consider coming and sharing a devotion or two. It would be good to have a woman along anyway. Right now it's just Pastor Ray and me, and we do have several girls going. We need a female chaperone."

"I'm not sure how I will handle sleeping on the ground."

"I'll get you a cot if you want. And your own tent. It'll be just fine."

Marissa tried to dismiss the idea of camping to embrace what the park had to offer the teens, especially those who didn't know the Lord. And she could stay a few extra days at the lodge for a time of personal reflection. It all sounded so appealing, she could barely contain herself.

"So what do you think?" he asked, rising to his feet.

"Are we leaving?" She looked around.

"I'm just going to get us some cheesecake. Got to have dessert."

"Sounds yummy." Marissa looked down to see her half-eaten sandwich wrap. "Or maybe we can split a slice?"

Again came a grin lighting his face. Was the suggestion too intimate, asking if they could share a slice of cheesecake? Did that mean they were ready for the next step? He soon returned with a nice portion covered in strawberries, along with two forks. She continued to eat her sandwich while he took a few bites, then passed the rest her way.

He suggested a possible menu for the retreat and asked

Marissa her opinion. She said spaghetti would work, thinking she might even be able to cook that kind of meal over a stove she'd never operated in her life. "Okay, count me in. So long as I can have a cot to sleep on. I don't want bugs crawling all over me." She flinched at the image of a spider dangling in her face.

"I won't allow one hairy appendage near you. But bugs are unfortunately a part of the camper's life."

She tried to eat a portion of the delicious cheesecake but found her appetite stymied by the thought of bugs. And then she thought she sensed one crawling on her arm. She shuddered and pushed the plate toward him. "It's yours. All I can think about is bugs."

He grinned and polished off the rest. "You'll do fine. I guarantee it."

Marissa liked his confidence. But she also liked the idea of basking in the beauty of Bryce Canyon. That meant more to her than anything. It would be a true start again on life. And who better to do it with than Anson?

ﺬ

Marissa was now in a dilemma. She looked through her wardrobe, wondering what she was supposed to wear on a camping trip. She'd only been on one such adventure as a lowly teen many years ago. Back then it was shorts and T-shirts for the day and sweats for the evening. The majority of her clothing these days consisted of nice pants, tops, and capris. She had knock-around shorts that might suffice. She owned no hiking boots and hoped sneakers would do the trick. She looked over the things spread out on the bed, including the bottle of insect repellent on top of the pile. With the trip extended into an extra two-day stay at the lodge after the church retreat, she would need plenty more clothing than just for camping.

She dragged out the suitcase and put everything in it—shorts, pants and tops, underwear, a dress, a hoodie, a pair of sneakers, and several pairs of socks. For a moment she wanted to call Anson and get his take on a wardrobe, though guys usually didn't have much opinion on the topic. Except Anson did know everything about the great outdoors, having a job within the national parks. She picked up her cell on a whim. When he gave her a few ideas, she thanked him and turned her attention to surviving the camping part of this trip.

Mom peeked in then and gasped. "Heavens, Marissa. You're only going for five days. It looks like you're moving out." She caught herself. "You're not moving away, are you?"

"No, no. I mean, one day I will when I have the money to pay the rent. Oh, and you don't have to worry about Sammy while I'm gone. A friend is taking care of him."

Marissa was glad they'd convinced Anson's friend Carl to babysit their respective pooches while they were away. Carl took it on reluctantly but smiled a bit more when Anson promised him a huge steak dinner as payback. Anson must think the gift of food paid everyone's bill, remembering how he promised her dinner for taking care of Goldie. They had a nice lunch instead, but she wouldn't mind a fancy candlelight dinner one evening, along with a walk in the sunset.

Mom interrupted her thoughts. "I just hope you're careful out there. Who else is going besides the kids?"

"The pastor of the church, Pastor Ray. And Anson—the guy who came over here to pick up Goldie." She hesitated, thinking of the engagement photo on the bookcase and her mother's reaction. She winced.

"You mean the one who looks like Eric?" Her mother shook her head. "Really, Marissa. I don't know what to think."

"Our friendship has nothing to do with the fact that he has the same hair color as Eric. It's no big deal."

Mom paused and then asked why no other women were going as chaperones.

"I'm not sure. I hadn't thought about that."

"Well, you really need another woman going. You alone with two men and all those kids. I just don't know."

Marissa hesitated. "Okay. I'll find out." When her mom left, she was on the phone with Anson once again.

"So do you have the wardrobe figured out?" he joked.

"I think so." She rattled off her selections.

"You remind me of Lucy and how she would agonize over what to wear each day to school. It was kind of funny. And the bed would be loaded with clothes."

Marissa decided not to mention the multitude of clothing strewn across her bed. "Actually, Mom reminded me of something. Am I going with just you guys?"

"What do you mean 'just us guys'?"

"You and the pastor. I mean, it would be good to have another woman along, and I kind of agree."

"Actually, I think you're it as the female chaperone."

She sighed and sank down onto the bed. "Then I probably shouldn't go, Anson."

"What? Marissa, please don't say that."

She heard an audible groan, as if this was the worst news she could have possibly given. A part of her glowed at the thought that he cared so much and wanted her along, even if she didn't have any camping credentials to her name.

"I'll call you back," he said.

"Anson?" The call terminated.

She looked at her cell phone, pondering it. Maybe she was just being paranoid over the single woman issue. Or maybe just being careful to guard her heart as she knew the Lord would want, especially with impressionable teens whose hearts and minds were open to anything and everything.

Her cell phone suddenly vibrated in her hand, making her jump.

"I left out an important detail." His voice escalated with excitement. "Pastor Ray's wife is coming along to help out. So you can still make it, right? I mean, don't worry about what you're wearing and everything else. You'll do fine and—"

"It's okay, I'm still coming. And I've met the pastor's wife, Alicia. She's very nice."

He blew out a sigh. "Whew. Okay, great. You had me worried. See you in about an hour."

She smiled, both at his relief and at how God was orchestrating everything so far. But most of all, her heart warmed at the thought of Anson's eagerness to have her along. *God, I give this all to You. Let it be a time of knowing Your will as You once showed me long ago when I was young. Help us reach out to the teens and show them the beauty of Your creation. And. . .if there is something happening between Anson and me, make Your will known in our lives. Amen.*

eleven

Anson greeted her with a huge smile and his large blue eyes when he drove up. The rear of the car was loaded with three teens, whom he introduced as Karen, Pat, and Jay. Karen and Pat issued hearty hellos while Jay only nodded his head and then looked at the small gaming device he held. Marissa managed a smile and slipped into the passenger seat while Anson struggled to place her large suitcase in the trunk.

"Looks like you brought everything," he commented when he returned, supplemented with a smile. "But I don't care. So long as you're here."

"I brought what was practical. And I'm glad to be here, too, thanks." She settled in her seat and looked back at the teens. "Did you have trouble packing, Karen? I think I had every piece of clothing I owned on my bed today."

"Oh, no. I love camping. I got everything into a small duffel bag."

Her confidence suddenly made Marissa feel a bit lower than the road beneath the car. "I hope I can figure this out," Marissa mumbled to Anson.

"You'll do fine," his soothing voice responded. "Not everyone's been camping."

"What about the pastor's wife?"

"Oh, Alicia hikes and everything," said Karen from the backseat. "They're really into the outdoors. She's even done some of the trails out in Oregon."

Super, Marissa thought, sinking even farther down into her seat. *Next to her, I'll feel like a Barbie doll.* Anson didn't have a tried-and-true chaperone to help him but just another kid in need of instruction. For now she tried to dismiss it and concentrate on what this would mean to the teens rather than thinking about herself.

At the visitor center, they stopped to wait for the van carrying the rest of the team. When they arrived, outfitted in rugged hiking apparel, Marissa glanced down at her starched cotton pants and top. She tucked her hair behind one ear and greeted Ray's wife, Alicia.

"We're going to have a great time," Alicia said. "I'm sure you've been here, right, Marissa? Most have that I know of."

"Well, a long time ago as a teen. I've been looking forward to visiting again."

She nodded, then waved the kids over to their respective vehicles. Marissa wished confidence ruled the day. Maybe she'd made a mistake volunteering to come along and be a part of this. She should have made her reservations to stay at the lodge and then hung out at the campsite and overlooks. But the lodge was expensive. The two nights she had reserved after the campout were plenty on her meager budget.

The caravan stopped at several scenic overlooks to take in the splendor of Bryce Canyon. Marissa marveled at the fascinating formations that were the canyon's trademark, along with its variegated colors, from gold and red to pure white. "Beautiful," she murmured. As a presence drew close, followed by a warm touch on her arm, goose bumps rose in response.

"I've seen the canyon so much, but I never tire of it." Anson gazed at the view from over her shoulder. She looked behind her to see his darkened face, shadowed by the sun. She couldn't tell what else he might be thinking. Or if he stared at her in a certain way. But now there was the retreat to consider and not other feelings that might be emerging.

Everyone piled into the vehicles and proceeded to the campground. Anson instructed the kids on how to set up the tents. Alicia grabbed a small nylon bag and strode over to a corner of the campsite. "This is our tent, Marissa," she said and began setting up a very tiny pup tent.

"I. . .uh. . . ," she began. "Wow, it's kind of small, isn't it?" And for sure it would never hold the cot Anson promised to bring.

"It fits two people just fine." She then took out a rolled blue foam pad.

"Anson was supposed to bring me a cot," Marissa said doubtfully.

Alicia chuckled. "A cot! You won't be able to get a cot into this tent."

"I guess not. . . ." Her confidence was leaking out quicker than faith could cap it off.

Alicia then brought out another foam pad. "I have an extra pad. You can use this if you want."

"I had Alicia bring one for you," Anson now said, venturing up to them. "I know I told you there'd be a cot, Marissa, but I thought the pad would be fine for two nights."

At that moment, she pondered the comfortable mattress and white sheets in a fine room at the Bryce Canyon Lodge. She said to Anson in a low voice, "Maybe I should rebook the rooms at the lodge for this weekend instead of Sunday and Monday nights."

"Why?"

"I can't sleep on the ground like this."

"Sure you can. And you're not directly on the ground. You're in a tent and on a pad. Alicia is great; she'll make you feel right at home. Take it easy." His gaze then drifted to the flock of teens. He lowered his voice. "You're going to need to go with the flow, Marissa. We have curious teens here who are watching everything. You'll do fine."

Marissa bit back any further comments and put on a fake smile for the group's benefit. She dragged out the huge flannel sleeping bag that Mom found in the attic and squatted down, wedging it beside Alicia's strangely shaped bag that could barely fit anyone. When she crawled out of the tent, Anson was giving directions for dinner preparations on a small stove connected to a green fuel bottle. Marissa shivered and went to dig out a fleece hoodie, thinking more and more of her inadequacy in this venture. Even at dinner when she sat with the other adults, she sensed a distance between her and the rest of them. They sat companionably together, planning the rest of the retreat, while she remained quiet.

After dinner she went to look for sticks to feed the evening campfire. Anson soon joined her. "You've been quiet. Is everything all right?"

She shrugged. "I don't know. I feel like I don't belong here."

"Of course you belong. I know you can do this, Marissa. You have many qualities the teens need." He touched her arm. Oh, how she wanted to feel his arms cradling her, imparting reassurance. She nearly threw herself into his embrace but held back.

Instead her gaze drifted to the teen group that gathered around the fire and then to the young guy named Jay, sitting by himself, staring off into space. She nudged Anson's elbow. "What's up with him? Why isn't he participating?"

"Not sure. I might have a talk with him later. God does different things in these kids, and they respond differently, too. Maybe he's a bit homesick. Or just feels out of place."

"I totally understand. I'm already homesick for my warm bed." She ignored his look and joined the circle of teens, eager for the fire's warmth.

Flames of light danced on the faces of the teens as they poked sticks of marshmallows near the glimmering embers. While they ate the gooey remains, Pastor Ray asked the group what they hoped to gain by coming on this trip. Marissa was eager to hear their responses as she settled down at a nearby picnic table to listen. She heard things like taking a walk among the hoodoos, seeing God answer a prayer, and finding out what to do with one's life. And then Jay's response: "To ask why I'm alive."

"That's important to consider, Jay," said Pastor Ray. "What is our purpose for being put here on this earth? Anyone have an answer?"

Jay's response made Marissa think of Anson. Why, she didn't know. She looked over to see him prying a melted marshmallow off a stick. Why were any of them alive at this moment in time? Why did God choose some, like Eric, to join Him early in His heavenly realm and yet leave others here?

The teens were quiet until Karen spoke up. "Pastor Ray, that's easy. God put us here to love and worship Him. It's what we're going to do in heaven, so we might as well get a head start."

Marissa couldn't help but smile. A great response, worthy of pondering in her own walk with the Lord. They all must work out their faith with fear and trembling while here in this world, to walk with God and not against Him, seeking His will in all things. And suddenly she was on her feet, spilling out these truths to the group along with her testimony. "And God has great things in store for each of you. Just keep your minds and hearts open to Him, especially while you're here."

All of them were staring at her. She sat down sheepishly and stared at the flames of the fire.

"Marissa has made some great points," Pastor Ray said. "Good things to think about as we spend time here. Now, is anyone interested in playing some games?"

The teens quickly became engaged in a few board games, while Marissa continued to babysit the fire, throwing on a stick to feed the hungry flames. Again there came that familiar personal warmth drawing close.

"You weren't kidding when you said this place did things for you," Anson remarked, sitting down next to her.

"I just want the kids to know that God loves them, and He has a plan for their lives."

"I was able to talk to Jay, Marissa. He just found out he was adopted, so he's taking it kind of hard. He really wants someone to listen. Kids need that. Not so much pat answers to everything, but someone who will stop what they're doing and show that they care."

On the heels of this revelation, Marissa saw Jay wave at Anson, asking if he would like to play a card game.

"See what I mean?"

"That's great, Anson."

As she watched them together, engaged in the game, she realized miracles were already happening. And now she looked around the campsite to see who God might knit her with. And suddenly her feet were propelling her toward Karen. God had a way of surprising with the unexpected. And she didn't want to miss out on being a part of His big plan here at Bryce. This wasn't just about her, after all. It was also about others.

❧

The weekend went by so fast; Marissa could hardly believe it was Sunday afternoon. She stretched her cramped muscles, reaffirming after two nights that she was not the ground sleeper Alicia and Anson hoped she'd be. But that was okay. She'd helped cook a nice meal last night with Karen, and now she and Karen were getting along well. Anson, too, had developed a friendship with Jay and promised to get together with him again.

Marissa was pleased for having survived the trip but, most of all, pleased that everything went well, as she and Anson worked together to minister to the teens. But now came the time of separation. Pastor Ray and Alicia would drive the teens back to Cedar City in their two vehicles. Anson would go his merry way with his job in the Park Service. And Marissa would spend a few days at the lodge on a personal retreat. Anson would then return Tuesday evening to pick her up.

Marissa helped the teens stuff their sleeping bags into tiny nylon bags and put the gear into a cartop carrier. Karen ventured up to give her a hug farewell.

"I'll have to visit you at the soap shop sometime," she said. "I love that place."

"Come around noon, and I'll take you out to lunch," Marissa promised.

The young teen's eyes lit up. Marissa smiled as Karen entered the van, crammed in with the other teens. When Marissa turned, Anson was standing apart from her but staring with his eyes slightly widened and lips parted in a faint smile as if he enjoyed the scene before him.

"Guess I'd better get you down to the lodge," he said, picking up her suitcase. "So you survived. I knew you would.

And without a cot."

"I did, believe it or not. In a tent fit for tots. And on the hard ground." She rubbed her back. "A nice bed will do me good tonight. I'm pretty sore after it all. Too much pampering in my life, I guess."

"Sorry about the cot and everything, but I'm glad you hung in there."

"It was fun. In a painful sort of way." She entered his car, and suddenly the words weren't there. Why, she wasn't sure. Maybe because the friendly people surrounding her all weekend had acted as a buffer between her and Anson. Not that she disliked being with him. On the contrary. But now alone, without the pastor or the teens, she was left with her feelings concerning him. Anson said little as well as they drove down the park drive to the lodge, almost as if he, too, were timid and thoughtful.

"So where are you this week, park wise?" she finally asked, hoping to talk about something rather than enduring the stillness in the car.

"They have me back checking out some visitor issues at Zion. I need to be there early tomorrow, so I plan to head over there tonight." He paused. "I wish I could spend more time with you, but. . ."

"Of course you have your job. This is my time to be with God anyway."

"We all need that. I'm alone days with the long drives to the parks, so I have plenty of time to think and pray."

How she wanted to know what filled Anson's mind and his heart during all that driving. Was it thoughts of the past and plans for the future? Could she possibly be in some future equation? After spending the weekend with him, watching him interact with the teens, and especially Jay,

Marissa liked Anson's characteristics more and more. He had both the compassionate and adventuresome sides that made an attractive picture. As well as displaying a merciful heart.

He drove up in front of the lodge. "All set?"

"Yes. Thanks for the ride."

"See you Tuesday night."

She nodded and rolled her suitcase up to the doors before turning to watch him drive off. She was alone. Of course there was plenty to see and do. The beauty of the park was at her beck and call. But without him, there was something strangely absent, like a part of her was missing. *Lord, I pray You do a work in my heart during my time here.*

After settling into her room, Marissa took a walk to a nearby overlook. Already early evening, the crowds had greatly diminished. At Sunset Point, she observed the Bryce Canyon amphitheater in all its glory, including the famous Thor's Hammer formation. Marissa marveled at it all and took time to search out every unique aspect of the canyon.

The teens had come here on Saturday, and Anson gave them a talk about the canyon and how scientists claimed it was formed. He supplemented it with a discussion about God's hand in creation. Marissa thought he would make a good science professor. Standing there at the overlook, she could still picture him—his large hand acknowledging the expanse of a red-and-gold-colored canyon, his voice heightened with excitement. The vision continued to stir her heart in a way she didn't think would happen so soon. But for now, she must settle these loud thoughts of Anson and, instead, concentrate on what God might be saying.

The next day, Marissa spent the morning at an overlook with her Bible in hand, studying scripture and writing thoughts in a journal. She once kept a journal back in college when the pressures of life caused her to seek God's guidance. She thought back to the important entries made during college, like the first time she laid eyes on Eric in her chemistry class. The dates. The ski trips they took.

Suddenly she was transported back to a snowy day on the slopes when she'd lost her way. Eric had skied up to help her. When he offered her a hand, they both found themselves in the snow instead, laughing. She might have thought love was born right there. Eric had also been intellectual and more of a homebody. Except for his fascination with skiing, he stuck to home, his computer, and his work. He liked being in Omaha, surrounded by family and friends, when not lured by the call of the slopes that he loved with a passion.

And then she thought of Anson and the activities they had done together in just a short amount of time. Walking their dogs in Cedar Canyon. Handing out bottles of water at the July Jamboree. Helping minister to the teens. Marissa bent over the journal and began to write. Thoughts of Anson filled her. The pleasant conversation. His smile. The touch of his hand on her shoulder. His face illuminated by the campfire the other night as he laughed with the teens. She had moved on with life. But now she wondered, as she drew a heart in childlike fashion in the margin of the paper, if she was also ready to move on with love? And did Anson feel the same way? Or was it too soon to even consider such a thing?

She closed the journal and took in the view before her. It appeared like a painting with hoodoos like miniature stone statues aligned in rows. They could have been an army of soldiers ready for duty or tree trunks without their limbs. Even an old city from biblical times, with caves for dwellings. But this was a land God had created. And the same place where He once breathed into her heart a desire to know

Him. Not in book form or in church form but in the reality of what He'd created her to be. His child.

Marissa stood to her feet, her heart at peace. Now a longing rose up within. She felt in her pocket for her cell phone, wondering if it was too presumptuous to call Anson and ask how his day was going. She'd had his information keyed into her phone log ever since he'd given her his business card. She hesitated before pressing the key.

"Hello?"

"Anson? Hi, this is Marissa."

She heard static and then one or two words. She walked down the trail, hoping for a better signal. Again came some mismatched words about Tuesday. Suddenly the signal was lost. Reluctantly she pocketed the phone, then walked around for a time before heading back to the lodge.

When she arrived, a matronly woman, dressed in the uniform of a maid, was sticking a note on her door. "Excuse me? Can I help you?"

The woman jumped. "Oh my goodness, you startled me!"

"I'm sorry. Did you need something?"

"Oh honey, I was just putting this note here. It's from Anson." She paused to stare at her. "You wouldn't happen to be that young lady he was telling me about? The one who'd lost her fiancé?"

Marissa blinked, wondering how in the world a strange woman would know that.

As if to answer her unspoken question, the woman hurried on. "I'm Diane. Anson and I are good friends. He told me about your situation. I was so sorry to hear about your loss."

"Thank you. It's been hard, but I've had help along the way. Family and friends."

"That's good. Anson is a wonderful young man. But I was

sad to see him troubled when we talked last. I wish I knew the words to say to him."

Marissa wondered what she meant. How was he troubled? By her? Was she doing something wrong by being so involved in his life?

"He's a dear, sweet man. And I know how important it is to take things one step at a time. Not to rush, especially when there's another man involved. And you need to find out, too, what you're supposed to do and who you're supposed to be with. You know what I mean? I used to say that to my boys. They didn't seem to want to listen. One got a divorce a year after his marriage. Another lives with his girlfriend."

Marissa's hands began to sweat. "I want to do what's right."

"Of course you do. Just be sure, if he's not the one you believe you should marry, that you let him go and not lead him on. Anson's a wonderful man. I guess I don't want to see him hurt but happy. You know what I mean? You're a bright, pretty girl. I know things will be just perfect, if they are meant to be." She smiled, said good-bye, and moved off down the hall.

Marissa was unsure what to think. She took the note off the door and wadded it up. All the feelings she'd experienced by the overlook—the scriptures, the memories, thinking God might be leading her heart, all the thoughts of Anson—were now replaced with questions. Was she doing the right thing? Was Anson the right man for her? Was she leading him on? Maybe she should pull back for a time, just to make certain of her heart and his. *God, I need Your timetable and Your wisdom. Not mine.*

twelve

The following day Marissa decided on a long walk—a journey of the heart into God's creation. The trail she chose took her below the canyon rim for a hike among towers of sandstone, drenched in the colors of red and orange. Some appeared like castles. Others made her feel insignificant, standing alongside these tall stones of strength and purpose. She would have enjoyed it more were it not for the conversation at the lodge yesterday. It must have been providential that Diane was there, right when Marissa arrived, to share her thoughts. After all, wasn't Marissa here to listen? Perhaps the words had come from God through the woman's lips to her ears. Gazing up at the rocky pinnacles, she asked once more to hear God's voice. Only the sound of the wind whistling through the canyon and rustling the sparse vegetation answered her.

A few hikers passed by, heading in the opposite direction. Marissa continued on until she came to a trail junction. She sat down to consider which direction to take. If only she'd thought to bring the brochure that described the hike. Her tongue ran across her dry lips, and she suddenly realized something else she lacked. She had no water. "Some hiker I am," she grumbled. *I can't seem to plan anything. Not my life, not even a simple walk.*

"Looking for a guide, miss?"

Marissa glanced up, the sun's rays shining in her face, to see a dark figure towering over her. When she stood, she recognized Anson in his park uniform. "Anson! What are you doing here? I thought you weren't coming until tonight."

"I went to your room and found out you were gone. So I decided to take a wander while waiting for you. Did you get my message? I left one at the front desk yesterday after our call broke up. I asked them to deliver it and to let you know I'd be in the park early."

The note. The one she'd wadded up after the conversation with Diane. "I didn't read it, sorry."

Anson shook his head, smirking. "I've heard of people being absentminded." He hesitated. "Is something wrong?"

"I. . .well, no." She knew it wasn't the truth, but at this point it made no sense to go into it. Instead she followed him up the steep trail as he described his time at Zion.

She paused to catch her breath while he seemed unaffected by the trail's challenge. "You're in good shape. You're not even winded."

"I hike a lot of trails. Goes with the territory." Again he paused to look at her. "I'm not sure, Marissa, but you don't seem yourself. Did something happen?"

He was beginning to read her emotions like a book. Better even than Wayne. "I'm fine."

He said no more but continued the trip through the cavernous rock. When they arrived back on top of the rim, Marissa was heaving. Her mouth was as dry as sandpaper. She watched Anson take out his water bottle and drink thirstily. "You don't have water with you?" he asked.

She shook her head. "No, and I'm dying of thirst, I'll have to admit."

"C'mon, follow me." He headed for the general store and to the back entrance where he hailed a worker. In a matter of moments, he presented her with two bottles of cold water.

"Thanks. I guess being an employee of the park does have its advantages."

"One time on a scorching day, I went down the trail with a daypack full of water. I gave them all out. I wondered how many of those visitors would have suffered heat exhaustion that day."

"You're like the cavalry, Anson. It's what you're good at." His head tipped slightly to one side, perusing her. She quickly shifted topics. "So what did your note say anyway?"

"That I had Tuesday afternoon off and wanted to know if you might be free for dinner at the lodge? I still owe you a dinner, you know, for taking care of Goldie."

"We had lunch."

"Hardly the same thing. So are you free, or is your calendar full?"

He grinned as if knowing full well she had nothing else planned. But yet things still cluttered her mind. "I'm not sure, Anson."

His smile evaporated. "Okay, there is something wrong." He moved to a picnic table under some pine trees and sat down. "You have to tell me, Marissa. Was it something on the retreat?"

"Oh, no. I had a great time. I learned a lot. It's. . ." She looked off into the distance. "Well, I met an older lady at the lodge who knows you."

"You met Diane?"

"Yes. She was the one who delivered the note to my room. And she. . .well, she cares a lot about you. And doesn't want things to go wrong, I guess."

His face reddened. "Oops. I did tell her about you. She's like a mother to me. I don't have one now, you know. I guess she wanted to help."

"Maybe it would be better if we both. . .kind of slowed down."

"Slowed down? What do you mean by that? Like not having dinner tonight?"

"No. I. . .I. . ." She hesitated. How could she tell him that she wanted assurance in these matters of the heart? Proof that if she fostered a new relationship, it wouldn't be ruined, too. Like Eric's.

"Marissa, please don't let one person's opinion drive everything. Diane can be a bit nosy, but she means well. We'll take this one step at a time and see where God is leading. I'm fine with that."

She considered it before allowing her gaze to encompass his face. She was no longer seeing anyone but Anson—for who he was and all that God meant for him to be. "Okay."

"So do you want to go out to dinner with me? Or would you rather wait?"

"Dinner would be fine, thanks."

His hand found hers and squeezed it slightly. No further words were needed until they sat down opposite each other in the dining room. Anson talked about his work in the parks and the visitors he'd helped. A few times he called out to several people he knew—a waitress here, a fellow employee there. Marissa observed this with interest as she slowly ate her meal.

Afterward he suggested a stroll by the overlooks to see the final rays of the setting sun pour forth their glory into Bryce Canyon. They stood there, watching the fading sunlight turn the canyon into different colors. "This is the best time of day to come here," he said softly in her ear.

The warmth of his hand slowly embraced the small of her back. She didn't pull away but fought to remain still, hoping she wouldn't tremble. His arms drew her closer. The kiss began gently, like a testing of waters, then slowly strengthened. When she opened her eyes, he was still looking at her, though he'd stepped back with his hands now tucked into the pockets of his trousers. They said nothing for several long moments.

"Guess we'd better get going," he finally said. "I'm sure you need to be back for work Wednesday."

"Yes. My bank account can't take another night here."

"I kind of wondered how you were able to afford two nights. The rates are pretty steep." They walked the path back to the lodge.

"Oh, Eric had given me money back in Omaha and. . ." She stopped. "Never mind."

"Marissa, it's okay to talk about him. He was a big part of your life for a time. I read the obituary."

"What?"

His face reddened. "Just that I know you loved him a lot."

"Yeah, I did. Once."

He said nothing more.

&

Anson wasn't certain why he was doing it, but once more he had Eric's obituary displayed on his computer screen. And the words that played over in his mind. *And his beloved fiancée, Marissa Jones, who will miss him dearly.*

This doesn't mean he is her forever love, he reasoned. *Or that she will never consider marriage again. Only that she misses the man.* He shouldn't let it affect him. There was nothing in it to concern him but for an active imagination. But then Marissa doubted whether they should be together. As if were a bad omen.

The cell phone rang, disturbing his thoughts. Lucy. "Oh Anson, I just wanted to tell you, the gift basket of bath products was wonderful. I loved what you picked out. Or you and whatever lady picked it out, that is."

"Hi, Luce," he said absently, his fingers running over the keyboard. He drew away from the screen to concentrate on the call. "Glad you liked it. And I did get some good advice from Marissa, actually. She works at the bath store."

"Oh, the one you were telling me about at the Jamboree." She paused. "Sounds like you're on the computer, huh? I heard keys clicking."

"Yeah, just glancing at that obituary again. Wondering if I should go check out Omaha sometime." He chuckled.

"Hey, Anson. . . ," she began.

"There's nothing new here, of course. I'm just trying to figure out where Marissa and I stand with each other. One moment I think things are going great. Then there's another curveball thrown that I have to handle."

"I'm looking at the obituary right now, too," she said.

"I shouldn't be reading things into it. Like there's competition or something. I mean, the guy is gone. Though there is one other guy I should ask about. That psychologist friend of hers. But she hasn't mentioned him much lately."

"Actually there may be something to all this. Things you don't know." There came a lengthy pause.

Oh no. "Like what?" He tried not to tense up, but he did. The tightness ran down his arms and crept up into his neck. And then there came twinges of a headache at his temples. *Great. She knows something about Marissa and Wayne. That's why Marissa had all those doubts at Bryce Canyon.*

"I thought maybe there could be something. Especially when your friend Marissa said how much you looked like her fiancé. I thought, no way. Then I saw the name and city in the obituary."

Huh? "Luce, you're not making any sense."

"Anson, I made a promise to Mom long ago. She asked me never to tell you, but you really need to know. It's your right. Especially with all that's happened."

Anson's palms began to sweat. "Luce. . ."

"Look, I'll just come right out and say it. You. . .you were adopted by Dad and Mom. I was five when Mom and Dad brought you home from the hospital at Park City. I remember it well, though. You were so tiny and frail. You looked like one of my baby dolls."

He could barely draw a breath, as if the wind had been knocked out of him. "What? No way."

"It's true."

"How can that be? Mom told me how they had to keep me in the hospital and all for several weeks. I had some health issues and everything. . . ." Anson paused, feeling like the carpet had been ripped out from underneath him. "She—she had all the baby stuff. The baby picture, the little blue cap they put on the boy babies. . .the whole nine yards. It was all kept in that trunk in the master bedroom."

"Yes, that's true. But you were still adopted. Mom and Dad found out about you through someone at their church. They drove up to Park City, took one look at you, and immediately wanted you."

His gaze traveled to the screen. "So what does that have to do with the obituary?"

"It was a teen pregnancy. The mother had twins. She kept one twin and left the other at the hospital in Park City, which was you. The mother's name was Henrietta Clay."

The words on the screen glared at him. Henrietta Clay. Park City. "No way." He stood to his feet and nearly dropped the phone.

"Anson, we don't know for certain if this is your birth

mother in the obituary. It may be just a freak coincidence. But even if it is true, it doesn't matter. Dad and Mom loved you very much. And I do, too, even if you were an ornery little brother who always seemed to get his way." She tried to laugh, but it came out sounding like hiccups.

"But if it does turn out to be true. . ."

"Then that man in the obituary could be your twin brother." The words came out in a near whisper.

Twin brother? And that meant. . .Marissa was engaged to. . . my brother? He stood to his feet and began to pace. "Look, I need to go."

"Anson, wait. I know this is a major shock. But we love you. Mom and Dad loved you. I'm sorry they aren't here to tell you this. But you must believe it."

Lucy's words were like some far-off melody. He told her a quick good-bye and stumbled blindly around the house with Goldie by his side whimpering. And then he thought of the first meeting with Marissa at the canyon walk. Marissa. . . who nearly fainted when she thought she was seeing Eric. And in all likelihood she was, if it were true. . .that she was the girlfriend and even the fiancée to some past link he never knew existed. Another identity, even if he could not make himself believe it. He returned once more to the computer and printed out the obituary. He looked at the mother's name, alive and well in Omaha. A mother who had helped plan Marissa's wedding, of all things. His fingers crinkled the paper.

Anson glanced over at a family portrait sitting on the bureau, taken a few short years ago. He examined it carefully for the first time—of Dad, Mom, Lucy, and him. He realized at that moment he had nothing in common with them, save the last name. The family characteristics of dark hair and brown eyes. The dimple on the chin. The short stature. He didn't look a thing like them—with his sandy-colored hair, blue eyes, squared-off jaw, and six-foot frame. He had no connection to them. Not one drop of family blood ran in his veins. He returned to the computer and did a search until he found a yearbook picture of Eric. He didn't look that much like him, in Anson's opinion. Maybe this was all a mistake.

Now what was he supposed to do? He did the only thing he could do at the moment. Pray hard. And get his best friend Carl over to his place as soon as possible.

&

"You're not making this up, are you?" Carl searched Anson's face. "No, I can see you're not. Sounds like something you hear on the news. I mean, Lucy was only five when it supposedly happened. How would she know all the facts?"

"Evidently Mom told her everything before she died. There's probably documentation somewhere. Lucy will find it, no doubt. Wow, I wish she had been kidding. But it would have been a sick joke, for sure."

"Anson, I don't know what to say. Wow. The mere idea that your love interest may have been set to marry your twin before he died. . .I mean, talk about coincidences. In fact, it's surreal."

"It makes me think of a picture I once saw on the Internet, of a tin can half open and worms slithering out. Talk about opening up a can of worms. . .and more."

"So if you find out it's true, which it may be, what do you plan to do?"

"Do? I have no idea. I just found out about this an hour ago. A few minutes can turn your life upside down."

"Okay, yeah. So say you're adopted. Many kids are. I mean you had great parents. A great sister. All that is good. And it may be you love the woman who might have been in love with your brother." His face colored. "I see what you mean. It is a tough situation."

"The idea that Marissa knows my birth mother. Had active interactions with her. Can you believe this?"

"So I'm guessing you haven't yet told Marissa."

"How am I going to do that? As it is, we were already on fragile turf. Have been from the beginning. Now I know why." He began to pace once more. "You realize, if the truth comes out, I'll only be a resurrected Eric in her eyes. Back to life, just as the Bible says."

Carl sighed. "Eventually this is gonna come out. You can't keep it a secret. The pieces will fall into place. Once the facts are established, the sooner you tell her, the better."

"You mean the quicker everything explodes. And I don't. . . I don't want that to happen."

Carl managed a smile. "You love her a lot, huh?"

"Yeah, big-time."

He blew out a sigh. "I don't know, Anson. The ball is in your court. You've been given a shocker for sure. I'd first confirm this all with Lucy via documentation or whatever. Make certain of the facts. Maybe talk to Pastor Ray about it. See what the next step should be. But if it ends up being true, you're gonna have to level with Marissa. And then see what happens. You can't undo the past, but you can live for the future. So walk this out and see what happens."

Walk it out? How? He was now stumbling about blindly, ready to fall flat on his face.

thirteen

Marissa reminisced about the kiss shared at Sunset Point above Bryce Canyon. While the canyon had once served to bring her closer to God, now it was bringing her close to a man she still knew so little about but thought she'd known forever. And that was hard to understand. Maybe it was because of his similarities to Eric. But Anson was his own man through and through. His was one of determination. Of allowing nothing to come between them, especially the way he held her firmly in his arms. And she did not shrink back either but welcomed it. She'd come to Cedar City looking for a new start in everything, including love. And she had found it in ways she never thought possible.

She sat on the floor, staring at the cell phone, contemplating calling Anson. Already Wayne had called, trying to snag her for another round of coffee at The Grind. She'd politely refused. Suddenly the phone jingled. She swiped it up and answered breathlessly, hoping it was Anson. Instead it was a voice she hadn't expected to hear.

"Marissa, how are you?"

She nearly lost her grip on Sammy, whom she held in the other arm. She gently put him on the floor and stood to her feet. "Why, Mrs. Donaldson!"

"Please, you know you can call me Retta. How are you? We haven't talked in so long."

Marissa smiled at the warm voice of Eric's mother. She told her about her first weeks in Cedar City, the job, and her new canine companion. Then she wondered how to broach the subject of Anson. Would the woman think it too soon to be in a relationship after Eric's death? That it trampled the memory of Eric she had nursed for the last few years? "Also, I met someone. A really great guy here in Cedar City."

"Oh, how nice. I know Eric would want you to be happy. What's his name?"

Marissa breathed easier at her acceptance. "His name's Anson. He works in the national parks like Bryce Canyon. He's a really nice guy. We walk our dogs together." She added a few more details, nothing much, but enough to let her know that life was moving forward.

"I was looking over some pictures, which is why I decided to call you. First to find out how you are. And I've been thinking." She hesitated. "Reminiscing, I suppose. It was a long time ago. But I wonder. . .with Eric gone, if it might be good to find out. . ."

Confused, Marissa wondered what she was trying to say.

"I'm sorry. I know I'm not making much sense. I guess it doesn't matter now. You see, Eric was a twin. He—he didn't know. No one knew but his father and me. We never told Mark either."

Eric's younger brother, newly married and living in a suburb of Omaha.

"This happened before I met my husband Gene. I was a troubled teenager. I became pregnant with twins. My mother could help me with one of them. But we decided to give the other twin away. We left him at the hospital in Park City."

A chill swept through her. She opened her mouth to speak, but nothing came out.

"Eric never knew he had a brother. Or Mark a half brother.

Maybe now is the time Mark knew. And maybe we could somehow find that brother. My twin son."

"Eric has a twin somewhere," she repeated, thinking aloud. Suddenly words came back to haunt her. And visions. The meeting with Anson at the park when she thought she saw Eric. Her mother throwing the photo of Eric in her face, claiming they could be twins if they dressed alike. Marissa took to her feet and ran for her room, dragging out the photo album.

"Are you still there, Marissa?"

"Yes, I am. Sorry. I'm looking at pictures, too."

"I guess I caught you at a bad time."

"No. I just. . .I don't know what to say."

"I'm sorry. I shouldn't have said anything."

"No, I'm glad you did." But her thoughts were in motion. *It can't possibly be him.* She began to chuckle. *Right, Marissa. He was born in St. George, you know.*

"All I can say is, if by some miracle I do find him, I hope we can meet. And I hope he can somehow understand why I did what I did so long ago."

"I guess you can only take this one step at a time," she said slowly. Retta offered a few more comments, asked that Marissa stay in touch, then said good-bye. Marissa sat on the floor as Sammy waddled up and began to paw at the cell phone. How does one find out if there is any truth to a wild-goose chase? She pushed the pup off her lap and headed for her laptop. She searched here and there, and on a whim, looked for the McGruders in St. George. She found a listing. George and Patricia McGruder. Deceased, as Anson had said. Two children. Anson McGruder and Lucinda McGruder Green.

"There has to be adoption papers on file." She slumped

over the laptop. It made little sense to do this. He couldn't possibly be the one. There was nothing to substantiate it but a few physical similarities. She gazed once more at the pictures of Eric. She then compared them to a few she'd taken of Anson on her cell phone during the teen outing at Bryce Canyon. The similarities were few and far between now. It had all been her imagination from the beginning. "So much for that."

Sammy had stretched out on the carpet at her feet, ready for an afternoon doze. "Guess I should take the hint and let sleeping dogs lie. Thanks for the reminder, Sammy." Until she glanced once more at the names on the laptop. Did some more searching on Lucinda "Lucy" Green. And came up with a phone number in St. George.

❧

Anson could barely concentrate on his work. He tried in vain to center his thoughts, his visions, his plans solely on Marissa. If only there weren't fresh barricades set against this relationship. The barricades of twins, adoption, a mother who may have once been the future mother-in-law to the woman he loved. Couple this with the special encounter at Bryce. He would take Marissa there again if he could hold her hand, gaze into her eyes, and share another kiss. He touched his lips briefly in memory.

A chill swept over him. Now everything had changed in a moment's notice. So much for Marissa being at the point of accepting him. With all this coming to a head, he had no idea what the future held. *I have to leave that up to God. He knows better than me.* He tried to dismiss it as he began checking over a comparison of visitor stats for a study to be presented at a business meeting the following morning. But the God equation still lurked in the back of his mind. One plus one equals two. *God, what are Your plusses and minuses for me? Is Marissa the big plus I've been waiting for? And what about the minus that seems to be hanging over us? What is going to happen with that? Does it all add up to zero?*

All at once his cell rang. He answered quickly, not bothering to check the ID. A soft, feminine voice greeted him. He straightened, his hand tightening around the phone. "Marissa! Hi."

"I'm sorry to call you like this when you're working."

"You can call me anytime."

"Thanks. I really need to talk to you. I thought maybe you might be at Bryce today."

"No. Not today. But I would gladly make it today. Every day, in fact." Except. . .wow, do you realize you may have been engaged to my long-lost brother? He couldn't believe he was actually thinking this. It sounded so foreign to him, so inexplicable, like some tale told by a Hollywood flick. He should keep such thoughts bottled up. Especially when they had no basis in fact yet.

Her soft chuckle flooded him with warmth and made him yearn for another moment like the one they had shared at Sunset Point. Or maybe she would like to come here. Cedar Breaks was a lot like Bryce, though smaller. Mira and Sandy, the two rangers at the visitor center, would love to meet her. He and Marissa could talk, walk around the park, and maybe even share another kiss. And forget all about adoptions and twins and the whole show.

"Did you hear what I said, Anson?"

"Sorry, Marissa. Yes, I heard. I was thinking that maybe you'd like to come up here with me sometime and see Cedar Breaks."

"I've been there. Well, a long time ago. Anyway, when are

you coming back to town? I have something I need to talk about."

"I can be there tonight if you want. I'm only an hour away." He didn't tell her the rest of the story, that he had a big meeting the next day at the national monument headquarters over at Grand Staircase-Escalante. That could wait. Besides he was curious to know what she wanted to talk about. And then he realized he needed to talk to her, too. Though he had no idea how he would ever broach the subject of adoption and twins. He would leave it alone for now. "Are you okay?"

"Yes. I—I just need to talk."

"I'll be there around six p.m." When he hung up, a sudden wave of doubt assailed him. He didn't like the sound of her voice. There was no way she could know about his past, could she? Or was it something else? A new set of worries plagued him when he should be concentrating on the reports for the upcoming meeting. He tried his best to focus on his work, even as he kept one eye trained on the clock.

When the time finally came, he drove straight to Marissa's. She sat outside on the porch with Sammy in her lap, as if waiting expectantly. She hooked the leash to the porch railing and walked over to his car. "C'mon up to the porch and have a seat. I made some lemonade. Are you hungry? Did you have dinner yet? I can make up some sandwiches, too, besides what I have here."

He followed, barely able to contain himself. "I'm fine. Don't worry about it. So what's up? You sounded serious on the phone."

She said nothing but poured him a glass of lemonade. He shook his head when she offered fruit and cheese on a glass plate. It was a nice little spread, hardly illustrative of some difficult discussion to follow. She then took a seat and popped a grape in her mouth. "How was work?"

"Okay. I've got a huge meeting tomorrow though, at Escalante. Which means I have to finish my report and then leave at the crack of dawn to make it there in time."

Her face instantly fell. "I'm sorry, Anson. I should have asked if this was a good time or not."

Uh-oh. That did not come out right. "It's always a good time when I'm with you."

His comment made her blush, and he was glad to have rescued the conversation. "I—I talked to Eric's mother this afternoon. She called."

His hand froze around the lemonade glass. "Oh?" He barely choked out the word before he began coughing. She came up behind him and gently rapped him on the back. "I–I'm okay."

She stood behind him, waiting. After a few moments, she stepped back and returned to her seat. "She. . .she was pretty emotional. Told me a few things about Eric I never knew. He didn't either."

Anson said nothing, only waited for what seemed like an eternity.

"She said Eric was a twin. It was a teen pregnancy. She kept him, but she gave the other away."

Anson quickly put down the glass before he dropped it. Things were slowly starting to add up. "Marissa, I just found out I was adopted. In Park City."

"I know. Lucy told me about it. I—I called her. I had to find out. She plans to locate the paperwork to confirm it. But she seems pretty confident. So if it turns out to be true. . ."

Then I'd say you have similar taste in men. He let the comment rest in his brain and, instead, stared across the street at nothing in particular. He then looked over to see Marissa's probing gaze, one that left him uncomfortable. "Then we know, I guess."

"Eric's mom so much wants to meet the child she had to give away. It means a living link to the child she lost. She's such a nice lady. She's. . ."

He stood to his feet. "Yep. She made a choice, didn't she? Keep the good one and dumped off the damaged goods." He recalled then the health problems he'd had at birth, or so he'd been told. Ill and frail. It had come down to survival of the fittest among twins. And suddenly he was angry.

Marissa was, too. "Anson, that's an awful thing to say. She's heartbroken over what happened. And it's not like you had an awful childhood. You lived just fine. Your adopted parents loved you. Cared for you. It must have been a heartrending decision for her. She was so young. A troubled teen."

"Look, I need to get ready for tomorrow's meeting. I–I'll call you."

He dared not dwell on the distraught look on her face or her eyes staring at him. He stepped off the stairs and walked to his car. *Now what, Anson?* He couldn't answer his own question. Instead he entered his car and heard his cell phone beeping from where he'd plugged it into the car charger. He swiped it up to check the number. Pastor Ray had called. He listened to the voice mail.

"Sorry to bother you like this, Anson, but the young guy from the retreat, Jay, wants to talk to you. He just found out something about his birth mother. He thought you would understand. He trusts you. Thanks." Anson found a pen and scrap of paper and jotted down the phone number. *It never rains, but it pours,* he thought. Just as he'd begun to find out about his past, here comes a young guy with a similar problem. Could he handle it?

He punched in the number. The mother said Jay had gone to the diner to hang out with friends. Anson quickly headed downtown to the diner where the young people often gathered. He could easily make out Jay, hunkered down in a booth with his handheld game as if trying to shut out the world while his buddies talked around him. For an instant Anson realized he was like that young man. After hearing the news today, he'd tried to shut out those who cared, like Marissa. But now he could do something about it rather than wallow in self-pity.

He slid into a seat opposite Jay. "Hey, there."

Immediately the teen put down his gaming device. "What are you doing here, Anson?"

"Pastor Ray called. Said you heard some news."

Jay bent his head and said nothing.

Anson studied him—the red flush of his cheeks, the way his fingers moved across the buttons on his handheld game when clearly his mind was elsewhere. "I got some news today, too," Anson went on. "You won't believe it."

Jay's head popped up, and his eyebrows narrowed. "What kind of news?"

"I heard from my sister that I'm adopted, just like you. The mother was a teenager when she had me."

"My real mother lives in Park City. And now she wants to see me. I don't know if I should meet her."

Park City. The city name struck him full force. "Wow. Well. . .uh. . .I know it's tough, Jay. You need to search your heart. It was a hard thing for our mothers to do, you know. Give us away when they knew they couldn't care for us." He inhaled a sharp breath. "They—they had to make some tough decisions. And we can be glad that God kept us alive when our birth mothers could have done the terrible thing, like get an abortion. We had loving parents who adopted us and gave us everything we needed." He shut his eyes briefly, thankful for that. He was alive. And loved. More than he realized.

"But what will I say if I see her?"

"What does the Bible say to do?" *Yes, what does it say, Anson? Consider it.* The words came to him, words that even now ministered to his own searching heart. "Show God's love. Maybe thank her for giving you life. And for making the decision to have you. We're all adopted sons and daughters, you know. Not just here on earth. God mentions in His Word that we have received the Spirit of adoption in which we cry out 'Abba, Father.' We want to know our fathers here and our Father in heaven. God understands our situation much better than anyone. And He can make it all work out if you give it to Him and trust Him with it." Anson sighed in relief, thankful for those words, even if he'd spoken them. He needed to hear them just as much as Jay.

Jay nodded. "She's gonna call my mother tonight. They're gonna set up a place and time to meet."

"I think it's a good idea. It will settle all those questions you've had in your heart."

"So are you going to see your birth mother?"

Anson hesitated. "I don't know yet. I'm still trying to put the pieces of the puzzle together. Find out if the facts are true. But if God wants us to meet, then it will happen the way it's supposed to happen."

Jay nodded, and the tense lines running across his youthful face began to relax. "Thanks for talking to me, Anson."

"Anytime, Jay. I mean it. Take care. I'll pray for you." He headed out but not with the normal lift to his step. Instead he was weighed down by the very words he had spoken.

What would he do if he found out he and Eric were related as he suspected? Could he go to Omaha and face the woman who had kept Eric and not him? Could he show the love that he'd just preached about to Jay?

fourteen

"I've been so worried about you. You haven't answered your phone in several days."

Anson was surprised to see Marissa standing outside his home with Sammy on the leash. Goldie made a flying leap off his front porch, and the two dogs barked as if greeting each other like long lost pals. "They remember each other." He looked on until he could no longer ignore Marissa's probing gaze. "Sorry I haven't called. I was waiting for the right time to see you."

"The right time...," she began blankly.

"Yeah. You know there's a right time for everything under the sun. It's biblical."

He watched Marissa shift back and forth in agitation. "Anson, don't you dare leave me in the dark..."

"Lucy found the paperwork. In a safe locked away. It confirms it. The birth mother was Henrietta Clay of Park City. Now Mrs. Henrietta Donaldson of Omaha, Nebraska. In fact, Lucy even went ahead and called this woman. They talked quite a bit. I guess the call you placed to Lucy gave her the courage to go ahead and find out."

The only sound for a moment was the cool wind whistling around the house. A change in the season was definitely in the air, in more ways than one. He saw her shiver. "Do you want to come in? You look cold."

Marissa shook her head. He left to fetch his jacket. When he returned she was still in the same spot as if frozen in place. She did accept the jacket with shaky thanks. "Well, we kind of figured that would be the answer." She studied him for a few moments. "So were you identical twins? I'm not sure if you are. I mean, you do look the same, but. . ."

"I don't know about that part. But I was born later. Seems Eric came before midnight on February twenty-eighth. And I followed after midnight March first. So he's technically the older brother."

"Are you. . .are you going to talk to Mrs. Donaldson?"

"I don't know. It will be hard asking why she thought Eric good enough to keep and not me." He couldn't believe he still said it. There it was—a continued deep-seated anger. Why he had it, he didn't know. In fact, it was foolish. But it was there nonetheless.

Marissa sensed it, too, for she took a step backward and looked down at the sidewalk. Then to his surprise, she tugged on Sammy's leash and headed up the stairs of the porch to plunk down in a chair. He assumed she would have walked away. Each day he was realizing what a special woman she was. And Eric must have known it, too. Marissa was turning out to be one in a million. A woman of godly virtue and beauty. He ought to feel blessed if he were not struggling at the moment.

"I know this has to be tough, Anson. But it's also a miracle in many ways. I mean, if we hadn't met, if I hadn't had such a freak-out the day I saw you in that canyon, all these other things. . .none of this would have come out. And you would not know who you are. And Eric's mom would not have known what became of her other child."

Anson said nothing for a long moment. He realized he'd been spared in many ways. God had preserved him, maybe even for this moment in time.

"Anson, talk to me."

"Sorry about what I said earlier." He scratched Goldie around her ears. "I'm still trying to work this all out. I probably should go see her. I mean, she lost someone close. She had to go through tough decisions as a teen. It would be good for her to know that one of us survives."

"Anson, just remember. This was a teen pregnancy. She was a child herself. Scared. Lonely. You can't condemn her for what she did. At least she gave you life. And you had a good life. Still do. We live in this world for God, even if we are temporary residents. To make the most of what He has in store for us, and to do it all for His glory."

"Wow, look at the preacher lady." He cracked a grin.

She blushed and stared at the porch floor. At that moment, she was the most beautiful woman in the world to him. Were it not for the seriousness of their discussion, he would take her in his arms and kiss her appealing lips. *And you were once engaged to my brother. My brother loved you. My brother was going to marry you.* The thoughts cut him to the quick. *Can you possibly love me for who I am?*

"I never was much of a preacher," she admitted. "I kept my Christianity mostly to myself. But you've brought it out, Anson. You have a gift, reaching out to young people and others. I like what you do."

"And how about the man? Do you like him also?"

Now her flushed face and dark eyes centered on him. "Yes, I like the man very much. And his name is Anson. He's strong. Determined. Loves dogs. Walks a lot. Camps. Wears a snazzy uniform. Preaches up a storm. Should maybe do missions or lead a church someday. Reaches out to hurting teens. And anyone who works in Bryce Canyon is a bonus feature in my book."

Anson took her hand in his, marveling at its softness. She smelled sweet, of some bath product at the shop where she worked. "Okay. Then let me walk this out."

Her hand slipped out of his. "Just promise me you won't do it alone. If you can, ask Pastor Ray or Carl to help. We're supposed to bear one another's burdens."

He nodded and watched her carry Sammy down the steps and place him on the sidewalk. He'd been blessed by the love and concern of family and friends. He knew that. And Marissa had his best interests at heart. But he must seek peace and pursue it. Peace in the realm of closure so he and Marissa could enjoy learning all there was to know about each other.

≈

The next day Marissa was surprised to find Pastor Ray's wife, Alicia, at the front door. She hadn't seen her since the teen retreat. Upon hearing who the visitor was, Mom immediately invited Alicia in for coffee and a slice of chocolate cake. Alicia smiled politely and found a place on the sofa, but her gaze never left Marissa. She sipped the coffee and ate the cake while asking how Marissa's time had been so far in Cedar City. And if she had recuperated from the retreat.

Marissa looked to Mom, who began edging her way to the door. "I'll let you two talk," Mom said. "I've got a few errands to run."

Marissa sighed in relief, thankful Mom understood. Last night Marissa had decided to clue Mom in on the latest developments. After revealing that Anson was indeed Eric's twin, Mom gaped in shock. "I knew it. They look so alike." She marveled at the information. When she had recovered from the shock, she was all business.

"And now what, Marissa? What do you plan to do?"

"I'm going to leave that in God's hands, Mom. But I will tell you that I like Anson very much. And not because of what we found out the other day. He's very special in his own way. And God has brought us together."

"I thought all this time you and Wayne were getting along. Betty said. . ."

"Wayne isn't for me. I don't know why, but he makes me uncomfortable. Anson doesn't." She must have had some dreamy look at the mention of Anson, as Mom's lips had contorted into a frown.

"Well, at least this Anson lives in Cedar City. And he did seem like a polite young man when he came here looking for his dog. I like a man who respects others."

Marissa was grateful for small things. But now she turned her attention to Alicia. "The retreat was special. I wonder what the future holds, though. Especially with Anson."

Alicia laid the fork on the plate and put the dish on the coffee table. "Anson told Ray what happened. And right now they're on their way to Omaha. They took an early flight."

Marissa jumped to her feet. "What?"

"Anson didn't want you to know about it until after they'd left. It was something he needed to do. Ray and he talked it over, prayed about it, and we all felt it was the right thing after Ray talked to the birth mother."

That may be, but all Marissa felt was disappointment. She'd been left out of the most important event in his life. Anson was going to see Eric's mother. If that were not difficult enough, he'd decided to go without telling her. After everything they had gone through these past few months. . .Anson had chosen not to involve her. "I think Anson has this strange impression that I'm only attracted to him because of Eric. I just wish I could convince him. . .everyone, that's not the case. God has done something new here. Anson is his own person. A fascinating and interesting man." She sank back down into the sofa.

"I can see you care about him very much." Alicia supplemented her words with a knowing smile. "Not that you couldn't tell from the retreat, the way you both talked and stared at each other."

Marissa gripped the sofa pillow resting beside her, wondering if it had been that obvious to everyone. "I do love him, Alicia. I know that. I just wish. . ." She hesitated. "Maybe the trip to Omaha will get us through this." *Even if I'm not a part of it*, she added silently. Anson had warned her ahead of time he wanted to walk this out in his own way. And likely he didn't want to burden her any more than she already was. Even if deep down she wanted to share that burden with him.

"We want to see a good conclusion for everyone involved. So why don't we pray for them and for the journey?"

Marissa nodded, closed her eyes, and listened as Alicia offered a prayer of help and protection for the two men journeying to Omaha. "May Your will be done here, God. And we pray for forgiveness, reconciliation, and healing to come forth. In Jesus' name. Amen." When Alicia left that evening, Marissa sat back, relaxed, at ease about the situation for the first time.

≥≈

The next day Marissa tried to busy herself with her job at the soap shop, all the while wondering when she would hear from Anson. She chose not to call him just yet, not wishing to interrupt whatever might be happening in Omaha. She could only pray for a good outcome, as Alicia said. A satisfying ending, one a reader often wished for in a romance novel, where the man and woman overcome obstacles to embrace love.

She wanted that conclusion in her life. At one time, she may have thought she was robbed of it, but all things were working together for good, as scripture promised. Eric was in a better place. And Marissa was on the path God had placed her, on the road with the man she believed was the one for her. Even if Anson was going back to where she and Eric once lived and dreamed and had nearly gotten married. To see the woman who was Anson's real mother. She shook her head, wondering at it all.

The bells to the shop door tinkled, and Marissa looked up to see a tall figure walk in. He looked around until his gaze fell on her. She froze with her hand on a bath product on an upper shelf. She finally let go of the box and turned, tucking strands of hair behind one ear. "Hi, Wayne."

"So this is where you work."

"Yes, for now. And it looks like I might be kept on at least through the New Year, which is good news."

His lips were drawn into a frown, his gaze never leaving her. "Can we talk?"

Marissa looked around for her boss and saw her near the cash register. She gestured him to the back room. "Yes?"

"I really think you're headed for trouble, Marissa. I feel as a psychologist and a friend that I need to warn you."

"What are you talking about?" Suddenly she thought of Anson and wondered if Wayne had heard some dreadful news concerning Anson and the trip.

"Your mother told my mother what happened. How Anson and Eric are related. Marissa, I can tell you from a psychologist point of view that what you're doing isn't healthy at all. You're losing your identity to someone who is only a figment of your imagination. You've chosen an unhealthy path here, resurrecting someone in your mind who is dead. You've never really accepted the fact that your fiancé is gone."

The words buzzed in her brain like a hive of angry bees. "That's not true. . . ," she began, though the doubts were clearly besieging her, robbing her of much-needed faith. "I'm choosing to trust God and. . ."

"I didn't study all this for nothing. It's obvious you have unresolved grief. You need some serious counseling to overcome it, Marissa. It's the only avenue available to deal with this issue. In fact, I'm going to set up an appointment for you with a psychiatrist."

Marissa ground her teeth. "Let's get real about things. Maybe it's you who isn't being honest, Wayne. Like you've never gotten over what we had or didn't have back in high school. You're the one living in some fantasy world. Thinking we're still old prom dates who need to move on with a relationship that's really dead in the water."

His face hardened like clay in a hot oven. His whole body became rigid. "Now you're getting defensive."

"And you're not? Stop playing doctor for a minute, Wayne, and see what's going on here. I'm moving on with life. Yes, Anson and Eric were brothers. Yes, I lost Eric going on nine months now. But Anson is not Eric. He is his own man as Eric was his own man. And Anson is everything I could ever want and need in my life." She set her gaze to the floor, but she stood her ground. "Look, I know you were there for me when I first got here, and for that I'm grateful. But that doesn't mean I want anything more than a friendship. Obviously you won't allow that to happen. You want it all."

"Marissa, I value your friendship. Which is why I'm here to warn you—"

"Of what? What is there to warn me of? You have nothing to base this so-called diagnosis on except for some mothers in a craft club who thought they could plan out their children's lives. But I'm trusting God to work things out. He knows my heart better than you or anyone."

"Even if it might be causing irreparable damage?" He stepped forward. "Marissa, be reasonable."

"I'm the most reasonable person there is. And I'm willing to live with my decision. I only ask that you let me."

Wayne shoved his hands into his pockets. And then there came a look of longing in his eyes, as if he wished things were different. Finally he turned and walked out into the main showroom. Before he left the shop, he looked back. "I'll be here for you, Marissa, if you change your mind."

"If you want to stay friends, that would be fine. But any more than that, I can't give you."

The door to the shop closed with the tinkling of bells. She breathed a sigh of relief for her decision and the strength of her faith despite the sudden doubt that had tried to weaken it. And with it, her love for Anson had grown, even if he wasn't here to see it.

❧

Anson stood at the front door, which was decorated with a cheerful wreath of dried flowers. His palms were wet. He shifted back and forth, sighing repeatedly. He looked to Ray for help, and the man gave him an encouraging smile. He stood there, wondering what he would say. He knew already the woman was looking forward to seeing him. She had eagerly accepted the invitation for them to stop by, even if her voice was filled with emotion.

He knocked. The door flew open to reveal a modest-looking woman. Young in the face. Bleached blond hair and blue eyes.

"Please come in," she invited. He immediately noticed the fragrant aroma of fresh-baked cookies. She had laid out a platter of large chocolate chip cookies on the coffee table along with other finger foods.

"This is my husband, Gene," she said. Her hands were shaking.

Anson politely shook the man's hand and took a seat on the sofa. They all sat quietly while Pastor Ray made small talk. Then he saw the photo, a huge portrait of a smiling Eric. And suddenly goose bumps broke out. He stood to his feet and went over to examine the photo. "So that's him?"

"Yes," said the trembling voice of the mother. She walked over and stood beside him. "That's Eric."

"Were we identical?" The question burst out of him.

"I'm not sure. But you were twins. Oh, if you could only know." She paused. "I tried. I wanted you so much. But I couldn't. It wasn't possible and—"

"It doesn't matter. None of that matters now."

She opened her mouth as if to counter it, then looked to her husband. "Come and tell me about yourself." She led the way back to the chairs.

Anson did so, though he found it difficult making eye contact as he spoke. He needed to, but something held him back. He wasn't sure what. Maybe he should have let her finish what she'd begun earlier. . .telling him about the past and why she'd done what she did. He needed this to go well. To be a friendly meeting. But maybe other things needed to come out of this, also.

"I know you said it doesn't matter. . . ," she began again,

straightening in her chair. She looked him in the eye, and he met her gaze. "I was only seventeen and pregnant with twins. I was told, you see, that I couldn't carry both of you. I was told that one would have to be taken so the other could survive. My mother would not hear of anything like that, and I'm glad. But I knew, too, after you were born that we couldn't take care of you both. And you were sickly also as a newborn. You needed special care at the hospital. It made sense at the time."

"I understand why you did what you did." He could picture her back then, scared and alone with two boys, and one struggling for life. She could do nothing else but leave him at the hospital and pray for the right parents. And God had been faithful.

"I thought a lot about you these many years. I wondered what nice family had adopted you. What you looked liked. What you enjoyed. How school went. If you had friends."

Anson fished out his wallet then and showed her pictures of his parents, now gone.

"Aren't they wonderful people." She wiped a tear from her eye. "I'm so glad. If they were alive, I would thank them over and over for all they have done." She looked at him again. "And now. . .I can hardly believe, but you and Marissa are seeing each other. And it was totally by accident."

"Pretty amazing, I'll have to admit." He sighed, then added, "She's a terrific woman."

"Yes, she is. And I'm glad my son. . .well, both my sons, love her. She's sweet, kind, and devoted. And I am so glad she moved to Cedar City. You can't know how glad I am." She closed her eyes. "Thank you, Lord. It was Your perfect plan."

When she opened them, Anson was looking directly at her. And though he did not know her as a son should, he wanted to learn more of her. And to bring that part into whatever his future held. With that, he promised to remain in contact.

Anson finished the pilgrimage at the cemetery with Pastor Ray accompanying him. Looking at the marbled stone with Eric's name chiseled on it, he wondered what it might have been like to have a brother. To play football with, to hike, even to ski, though he'd heard from their mother of Eric's excellent abilities in that area. He saw a pot of flowers there. He wondered if Marissa still had a bond with this man, even in death. If it was something that could be overcome in the days ahead. Or if he would have to let her go.

&

"Well, this has been a quite a trip," Pastor Ray commented as they began the flight home. "How are you taking it, Anson?"

"I'm doing okay, Ray," he said with confidence. Sunlight streamed through the window of the plane. A new day had come, and with it, a new outlook on life. "It went better than I thought. I knew it would be tough, but I needed to do it."

"You can move on," Ray added. "Though you do plan to stay in contact, which is good."

Anson nodded. He wanted to move on, to change course, hoping it would lead him to Marissa. Marissa, whom he wanted to carry off into another spectacular sunset like the one they had witnessed over Bryce Canyon. She'd giggle in his ear, her hands around his neck, pressing her face into his, her hair scented with something from the soap shop where she worked. At their feet would be Sammy and Goldie. He only prayed that Eric's memory did not exist in the middle of it all.

"You all right?"

"Yeah." He paused, deciding he might as well get these thoughts out in the open, too, as he had with everything else. "I've been thinking of asking Marissa to marry me. I really love her very much. But now I wonder if it's a good idea, especially after all this." He glanced over at Ray, who stared back, his face deadpan.

"Well, I thought that's why we were doing this."

"Huh?"

"Why we were making the trip. Eric is in a better place. God is interested in us finding healing. And that also means moving on in His grace and in faith. Of course, Alicia and I would like it, too, if you could set up a few premarital counseling sessions with us. We recommend it for new couples looking to marry."

"I don't know if Marissa's going to agree anyway. With all this now out in the open, it might send her running in the opposite direction."

"To where? Anson, she has no other place to go but forward. Wait and see. I think you'll be pleasantly surprised."

When they landed in Salt Lake, Marissa felt so close even though they still had a several-hour road trip back to Cedar City. He could hear her voice and see her fabulous hair swept up by the wind, and her dark eyes staring into his. It was a vision that remained with him and, he prayed, a vision that would last.

fifteen

Life was a journey of unpredictability, as Anson had discovered. Twists and turns. Canyons and mountains. But with God, it could only lead to happiness. Anson was ready to open the door and receive whatever awaited him. He knocked, anticipating the wide-eyed look of surprise on Marissa's face before glee escaped her lips, her hair cascading over her shoulders. And then the feel of her arms around him as they embraced.

Instead, Mrs. Jones met him at the door with Sammy barking faintly in the background. "Marissa's at work. Something about doing inventory for the upcoming Christmas season. I wouldn't bother her at the store right now."

"Oh. Okay." He backpedaled until her voice stopped him short.

"You really do like her, don't you?"

Anson stared. His hands fumbled for the pockets of his cargo pants. "I. . .she's a wonderful person, Mrs. Jones. A caring and gentle woman. She wants to make others feel good about themselves. She loves God and wants to do His will. She seeks Him in everything and in every situation. And I know she loves you."

Rosie Jones stood there quietly. He wondered if that was a tear hovering in the corner of her eye. "I hope she does. I think she believes I'm just a mean old lady. But all I have is my daughters. I want what's best for them."

"As do all mothers, Mrs. Jones. I'm sure Marissa knows that."

"I'm not sure she does. I know I can be hard. Maybe I have some unforgiveness for her leaving like she did. Which wasn't her fault. She was following what she thought she should do. I shouldn't blame her for my unhappiness."

Anson stayed quiet, uncertain how to respond.

"But you seem like a nice man. I must admit, I was so amazed to learn you were Eric's brother. Marissa told me, you see. Maybe it would have been better for me to have gotten to know him. I mean, it's too late now. But at least I can get to know you."

"That would be great, Mrs. Jones. I'd be glad to be a personal escort, too, whenever you want to visit one of the parks around here."

She smiled. "And that dog of yours—well, I'm not a big dog lover, but that dog Goldie was very sweet. She followed me everywhere. I think once Marissa leaves, I might look into getting a golden retriever for myself."

Anson smiled. "I'd be happy to help train the new dog you end up getting, Mrs. Jones."

"Thank you. That's sweet of you." She hesitated. "Would you like a lemon bar? They're Marissa's favorite." She went back inside and soon returned with a paper plate of bars in a Ziploc bag.

"Thanks. It was nice talking to you."

"And you. Good-bye." For the first time, he saw her smile. And with that, a smile formed in his heart, and a confirmation, too, of what his heart had been speaking. He only hoped Marissa felt the same way.

❧

Marissa's cell phone rang early that afternoon. It was him at last. Marissa could barely handle her phone, her hand was shaking so. "Anson? Oh Anson, I've been waiting to hear from you! Why haven't you called me?"

"I'm sorry. I—I wanted to wait for the right time and place. Did Alicia tell you?"

"Yes, she did." Marissa waited, switching the phone from one ear to the other, her curiosity beyond her control to keep still. "Anson?"

"I'll tell you more when I see you. But I can say that it went well. Very well, in fact. And I was glad Pastor Ray was with me."

"Oh Anson, I'm so glad!" Tears sprang into her eyes. Tears for everything and especially for him. She could hear him breathing over the phone and wished her arms were holding him right now, his face pressed close to hers, feeling his warm breath fanning her cheek. Even on the phone he felt so close, she could nearly touch him. "When. . .when can I see you? After I get off work?"

"I'll pick you up."

"I'm off at four. Don't be a minute late." She could hear the grin in his voice as he promised to be right on time. When she clicked off the phone, four p.m. could not come soon enough.

❧

Marissa could barely get through the rest of the day, her mind buzzed so. She paced continuously around the shop, looking for things to do, no matter how mundane. After the count was complete, she picked up a feather duster and began swiping away specks of dirt. Even her hands trembled along with the rapid beating of her heart.

"I can tell you can't wait to see Anson," Mrs. Holden observed.

Marissa whirled. "You know he's back?"

"I talked to Rosie at noon. Anson stopped by your house this morning."

The feather duster swiped a glass canister of bath salts, sending it crashing to the floor. The glass shattered. "Oh, no! I'm so sorry, Mrs. Holden."

The woman only laughed as a strong scent of lavender filled the shop.

Marissa quickly fetched the broom. "You can take it out of my pay."

"Don't worry about it."

"I wonder why he didn't come by then to see me. I mean he did call, but. . ." She thought it odd he would see Mom but not her. Had something occurred in Omaha that made him reluctant to stop by? Or had Mom said something that might have put a barb in their relationship? She swept up the salts into a dustpan and dumped it in the trash.

"You'll see him soon," Mrs. Holden said matter-of-factly.

"I guess." She dearly wanted to ask Mrs. Holden if she could leave early. It was all she could do to contain herself. Yet when the time came, instead of expectation, Marissa was tired. Weary of everything. Of life's issues, especially. She dragged herself out the door, trying hard not to cry when she spotted a familiar SUV parked outside.

"Going my way?" a voice called out the window.

How she wished she could be cheerful when she saw Anson's smiling face. Instead she only felt irritation on many fronts. "Why did you wait to see me? You went to see Mom and not me? Is something wrong?"

The smile disappeared from his face. "Sorry. I thought I'd let you do your work. Your mom said you were pretty busy."

"I would have made time for you day or night, Anson." Marissa wished herself to stay calm, knowing none of this was his fault. She finally slipped into the passenger seat and fastened the seat belt. "So where are we going?"

"Surprise. And don't worry, your mom is taking care of Sammy. This is our time to be together."

For a time she didn't know what to say. And neither did he. The situation had left them both speechless, on the hunt for the right words and emotions after what they had endured. At last Anson opened up. About the meeting in Omaha. Seeing Mrs. Donaldson. The promise to remain in contact with her. "She really cares a lot about you," he said. "Like the daughter she doesn't have."

Marissa smiled. "She is a nice woman. I'm glad, even if this was difficult for you, Anson. Even with her loss, she's gained a son. Not that you are Eric," she added quickly.

He stared at the road ahead. "And what about you? What have you gained?"

"A man who cares about me. And thinks of me more than just a friend from the school yard."

"I think I know what you mean. I've wanted that, too. Someone who cares, and someone I can care about. And one who doesn't think of me as, well. . .someone else."

If Marissa were behind the wheel, she would have brought the car to a stop. As it was, she pointed to the side of the road and asked him to pull over.

"What's wrong?"

"Plenty." Marissa leaned over, took his face in her hands, and kissed him soundly on the lips. "There. That's just to remind you who I care about, Anson McGruder. Okay, you may be the younger brother by two hours of the man I was once engaged to. But you're more than I could ever hope for."

Anson said nothing for a moment, as if paralyzed by the sudden encounter. "Uh. . .do you. . .do you mind if we keep going? We can make it in time if we do."

"Where are we going anyway?" She glanced around.

"Actually, I think have a clue." She settled back to enjoy the remainder of the drive and the man taking her to the place she loved most. Only she was curious to know what deadline he was trying to make. As they drove into Bryce Canyon National Park, she thought perhaps he had an evening meeting to attend. Or maybe another fateful encounter with Diane, the cleaning lady and his second mother, though Marissa couldn't imagine why. Instead he pulled into the parking lot near the lodge, just as the sun was beginning its descent toward the horizon. Bryce Canyon would soon reveal its inner beauty under the fading rays.

"Ah, I see what you mean by wanting to make it on time," she said, laughing as he opened her car door. They strolled the paths as they had once before, in another time, and watched the sun set.

"Is it any different now?" he suddenly asked her.

"If you mean, is it different from the last time I was here, yes. I was full of questions. I thought they might have been answered, but there were some doubts thrown in for good measure."

"You don't have doubts now? Even after everything's been revealed?"

"It's actually what makes the doubts nonexistent now, Anson. The questions are answered. Though I know it will take time for the both of us to get used to the idea of who you are." She allowed his arms to encircle her as they took in the sunset over the famous canyon.

"Then would you mind if perhaps we call on Pastor Ray and Alicia?"

She looked into his eyes.

"They offered some counseling sessions. For those who one day want to. . ." He hesitated. "I know we still need time to digest it all. Who I am. Who you are and were."

Her heart began to flutter. "Like in premarital counseling?" She saw his cheeks flush. Then a quick nod of his head. "I think that's a good idea, Anson. One step at a time."

"It's all we'll ever do. I promise. Whether it be the canyon walk, the Navaho loop walk in Bryce, or life's walk."

She welcomed the determination and commitment in his kiss. "Good. I can't wait to start!"

A Letter To Our Readers

Dear Reader:

In order that we might better contribute to your reading enjoyment, we would appreciate your taking a few minutes to respond to the following questions. We welcome your comments and read each form and letter we receive. When completed, please return to the following:

Fiction Editor
Heartsong Presents
PO Box 719
Uhrichsville, Ohio 44683

1. Did you enjoy reading *Heart of Mine* by Lauralee Bliss?
   ❑ Very much! I would like to see more books by this author!
   ❑ Moderately. I would have enjoyed it more if

   _____
   _____
   _____

2. Are you a member of **Heartsong Presents**? ❑ Yes ❑ No
   If no, where did you purchase this book? _____
   _____

3. How would you rate, on a scale from 1 (poor) to 5 (superior), the cover design? _____

4. On a scale from 1 (poor) to 10 (superior), please rate the following elements.

   _____ Heroine   _____ Plot
   _____ Hero   _____ Inspirational theme
   _____ Setting   _____ Secondary characters

5. These characters were special because? _____

_____

_____

6. How has this book inspired your life? _____

_____

_____

7. What settings would you like to see covered in future
   Heartsong Presents books? _____

_____

_____

8. What are some inspirational themes you would like to see
   treated in future books? _____

_____

_____

9. Would you be interested in reading other **Heartsong
   Presents** titles? ☐ Yes ☐ No

10. Please check your age range:
    ☐ Under 18   ☐ 18-24
    ☐ 25-34   ☐ 35-45
    ☐ 46-55   ☐ Over 55

Name _____

Occupation _____

Address _____

City, State, Zip _____

E-mail _____

MINNESOTA MOONLIGHT

3 stories in 1

When ideals, dreams, and plans are at stake, three modern women find it hard to trust the men who vie for their love.

Contemporary, paperback, 352 pages, 5¾6" x 8"

Please send me ____ copies of *Minnesota Moonlight*. I am enclosing $7.99 for each.
(Please add $4.00 to cover postage and handling per order. OH add 7% tax.
If outside the U.S. please call 740-922-7280 for shipping charges.)

Name _____

Address _____

City, State, Zip_____

To place a credit card order, call 1-740-922-7280.
Send to: Heartsong Presents Readers' Service, PO Box 721, Uhrichsville, OH 44683

Presents

Great Inspirational Romance at a Great Price!

Heartsong Presents books are inspirational romances in contemporary and historical settings, designed to give you an enjoyable, spirit-lifting reading experience. You can choose wonderfully written titles from some of today's best authors like Wanda E. Brunstetter, Mary Connealy, Susan Page Davis, Cathy Marie Hake, Joyce Livingston, and many others.

When ordering quantities less than twelve, above titles are $2.97 each.
Not all titles may be available at time of order.